CROSSROADS

OPERATION MARRAKESH
BOOK 5

BLAZE WARD

KNOTTED ROAD PRESS

Crossroads
Operation Marrakesh, Book 5
Blaze Ward
Copyright © 2024 Blaze Ward
All rights reserved
Published by Knotted Road Press
www.KnottedRoadPress.com

ISBN: 978-1-64470-504-9

Cover art:
Illustration 126123647 © Freestyleimages | Dreamstime.com
Illustration 27091513 © Marcin Zdrojewski | Dreamstime.com

Cover and interior design copyright © 2024 Knotted Road Press

Reviews
It's true. Reviews help. Even a short one, such as, "Loved it!" So please consider reviewing this book (and all of the ones you've read) on your favorite retailer site.

Never miss a release!
If you'd like to be notified of new releases, sign up for my newsletter.

http://www.blazeward.com/newsletter/

Buy More!
Did you know that you can buy directly from the Knotted Road Press website?

https://www.knottedroadpress.com/shop/

ALSO BY BLAZE WARD

The Jessica Keller Chronicles

Auberon

Queen of the Pirates

Last of the Immortals

Goddess of War

Flight of the Blackbird

The Red Admiral

St. Legier

Winterhome

Petron

CS-405

Queen Anne's Revenge

Packmule

Persephone

First Centurion Kosnett

Encounter at Vilahana

Consensus at Aditi

Hegemony at Dalou

Princes at Ewin

Empire at Gloran

Domain at Yaumgan

Additional Alexandria Station Stories

The Story Road

Siren

Two Bottles of Wine With A War God

The Science Officer Series Season One

The Science Officer

The Mind Field

The Gilded Cage

The Pleasure Dome

The Doomsday Vault

The Last Flagship

The Hammerfield Gambit

The Hammerfield Payoff

The Bryce Connection

The Science Officer Series Season Two

Alien Seas

Buried Among the Stars

Captain Navarre

Last Stand

Lost Dreams

Ghost Towns

Games People Play

Prophet and Loss

Dandelion

Emergency

Warchild

Moot

Doomsday Girl

Princess

The Coven

Preacher Man

Captain Daring

Revoked

Returned

Reborn

The Lazarus Alliance

Escape

Return

Rebellion

Revolution

Liberation

Retribution

Alliance

Shadow of the Dominion

Longshot Hypothesis

Hard Bargain

Outermost

Dominion-427

Phoenix

Princess Rualoh

PRELUDE

Log: Directorate Cruiser, Tactical Transport Marrakesh (CTT)
   Station: Horwin
   Attached Special Mission Modules
   A) Cargo
   B) Cargo
   Mission: Extended Exoarchaeology with Special Mission Shuttle
   Project: C51-C9O55M33
   Security Clearance: 2+

1

———————

Captain Padraig Boru smiled as he glanced over at Squire Taggart, seated next to him on the bench in the waiting lounge of the *A'Zedi* Intelligence Services main Bureau.

The benches themselves were hardwood, polished by generations of uniformed bottoms. The tile was old and showed indications that it had been handpainted in mauve, about one tile in five across the floor and waist-high on the walls. It brought him comfort, the way it and his dress uniform blended together.

Many of the same folks behind the counter. All civilians, in brown or blue for the most part, so that you didn't mistake them for sailors. Older, as well, generally middle-aged, with an air of composed sternness that hardly ever smiled.

A door opened on the far side of the counter and the Permanent First Secretary, Madam Mariami Gelashvili, stood there, smiling wryly as she spotted the two of them, alone on this side of the room, separated by a great barrier of old, polished wood.

"Captain Boru, Squire Taggart, if you would join me?" she asked.

Like that was a question, given that she had ordered them to arrive here today to discuss whatever *Marrakesh*'s next mission was.

Padraig rose. Nyssa Taggart had shaved her deep bronze head entirely, rather than having the buzzcut that was normally the minimum allowed. And she'd gone ahead and polished it with something to the point that it gleamed.

She also smiled more than she used to, so Padraig considered that outcome a win as he followed her down the row to the aisle and through the gap in the counter.

Madam Gelashvili's office hadn't changed since he'd last been in it six weeks before. Just enough time for *Marrakesh* to have a quick overhaul and the crew to all get some liberty after their most recent mission.

Lots more smiles there, as well. Padraig had the sort of crew these days where he expected to get jealous hate mail from his fellow captains.

Luck of the draw, certainly, but at least the Fleet had recognized that they had captured lightning in a bottle and left the crew mostly alone, though Padraig knew that he was due to lose some of his people in a year or less, unless some strings got pulled.

Tomorrow's problem. He followed Taggart into the office and they remained standing as the Permanent First Secretary settled.

"Be seated," she said amiably. "Boru, close the door."

He closed the door, then sat, settling as she watched them with the most bemused expression Padraig had ever seen on the woman. Normally, she was businesslike and professional. Today, she seemed on the verge of laughter.

"Sorry," she said after a moment. "Normally, the missions we send you on tend towards the serious, even dangerous end of things, Captain. This one might be rather a letdown for your crew."

"Personally, I prefer quiet missions, First Secretary," Padraig replied. "*Marrakesh* is a Tactical Transport. I prefer not having the weight of the entire Directorate on our shoulders."

"This one should be more tame," Gelashvili nodded. "But I needed to provide some background. Are you familiar with the field of cryptozoology?"

Padraig mouthed the word, but drew a blank.

"Cryptids, Madam Secretary?" Taggart asked. "Space vampires and that sort of thing?"

"I'm not entirely certain, Squire," the woman nodded. "However, I feel you are headed in the correct direction."

Padraig wondered if he was about to be part of some practical joke, but the First Secretary sobered and opened a file.

"There are certain elements of society that are perhaps less respected than others," she began, glancing up from the folder, but held it in such a way that Padraig couldn't read anything. "And yes, some of them verge madly down into odd conspiracy theories and expectations of creatures with no grounding in science whatsoever. That does not stop them from believing. Or at least grifting a good ducat along the way."

She paused and looked up. Padraig merely nodded and listened. This woman was the Permanent First Secretary of *A'Zedi* Intelligence Operations. The senior-most civil servant in the building, above whom were only political appointees who came and went.

"Intelligence maintains quiet threads of contact into that world," she continued. "Folks like that might be harmless, but they might also take some of their madness too seriously and need to be dealt with."

Padraig noted Nyssa's shudder at what *dealt with* might entail, but they were all spies these days, and some things you didn't talk about in polite company.

"In fact, we even solicit grant writers to apply, because that lets us keep tabs on things," their boss said. "Recently, something came up. More importantly, it appears to be interesting enough that it was brought to my attention. Something of a longshot, mind you, but even then, we maintain time and budgetary flexibility to explore such things. That's where you come in, Boru. How well do you know your ancient history?"

Padraig perked up. History hadn't ever been his thing in school. He'd thrived on mathematics and physics, originally hoping to make a career in the Navy as an engineer, until they'd slotted him into a command track.

"Probably not enough, Madam," he admitted. "Easily remedied, if you point me to the right source materials."

She nodded. Smiled even, like he'd passed some unexpected quiz.

"Before the *Sovereign Collective Directorate of A'Zedi*, there was *Riffrost*," she said. "Legally, the *United and Free Worker's Cooperative of Riffrost*. What we know of today as *A'Zedi*, *Traisa*, and *Wronlori* all spun off from *Riffrost* when it came apart, though even as late as that, the region that would become our *Directorate* was more of the barbarian swamps than anything. Still, the founding of *A'Zedi* came about because of *Riffrost* imploding."

"Yes, ma'am," he nodded.

That much he knew. Most students managed that.

"Before *Riffrost* was *Naara*," she continued. "The *Naara Mercantile Coalition* originally, but it had evolved into a rather nasty theocracy by the end. The outer portions of *Naara*, socially rather than geographically, rebelled and split off, eventually forming *Riffrost* and a few other places after a century or so of uncivil war, with the rump turning into what is today the *Holy Imperium of Copez*. We're talking a stretch of roughly nineteen hundred years from the original founding of *Naara* until now."

She paused.

"With you so far," Padraig nodded.

There would be more, but he could absorb this, turn Nyssa loose on the deeper details, and have someone recommend a couple of books he could read to become enough of an instant-expert on the topic for this mission.

That was the secret to command. Become that instant expert, then forget the details when you're done and move on to the next topic and the next mission.

"One of our contacts in that rather exotic and perhaps seedy realm claims to have been able to translate an ancient datacore that contains calculations for the current coordinates of a world," she said in a heavier voice. "Said world supposedly contains the remains of one or more ancient starships. Given the timeframes, it is presumed within my department that any such finds would be at a lower level of technological advancement than *A'Zedi* and our current neighbors maintain. However, we cannot be certain. The contact submitted a grant proposal to travel to this world and investigate. We've decided to escalate things significantly, because he envisioned some old tub of a freighter, leaking atmosphere and barely able to make Ghost-space to travel there. I'm sending *Marrakesh*, but you will continue to pretend to be old, worn, and the last of the *M-class* boats still in service. That lets you examine anything you find, Boru. And I trust your judgment to handle it properly, if it does turn out to be a problem, because you will be so far away from Horwin that signals will possibly take a week or more to get to me."

It was Padraig's turn to shudder. That was a lot of light-centuries to travel.

"Which direction?" he asked her.

"Spinward from *Traisa* somewhere," she replied. "Rimward from *Wronlori*. The middle of nowhere, on all our maps. That's all we have at present, as the gentleman in question isn't entirely willing to share more until the expedition is underway. Partly, that's his own personality. Partly his history."

"Oh?" Padraig asked.

"Professor Nicodemus Whitlaw," she nodded. "According to my files, an exiled *Wronlori* exoarchaeologist. Most recently, he's been living in *A'Zedi*, haunting libraries and parts of the social fringe, where he has managed to survive on donations, grants, bullshit, and the occasional consultation on fencing of stolen goods."

"Stolen goods?" Nyssa perked up.

"Looted antiquities," Gelashvili nodded. "You need an expert to identify such things and properly value them for sale. There is an entire black market subculture there, as well, which is why

Intelligence Operations maintains those contacts. You never know when something interesting might come up."

"And this might qualify?" Padraig's confirmed.

She nodded. Then shrugged.

"We can't be sure," she admitted. "It does, however, look good enough to send an old transport overloaded with food to investigate, with the understanding that it might turn into a full archaeological dig at some future point, with major universities getting involved and government backing. I rate the possibility as one in seven, but even that one leaves enough uncertainty that it must be investigated. And you will be a significant distance from any safe base, operating on your own in areas that have not had any sort of formal census in decades if not centuries at this point. We honestly have no idea what you might be facing. A simple freighter might vanish without a trace if something happened. I expect *Marrakesh* to give a better accounting of itself if it comes to that."

"Understood, First Secretary," Padraig said. "Sounds like I have some homework to get ready. "When will this Professor Whitlaw be reporting aboard?"

The smile was back. He didn't like it.

"That's the interesting part, Captain," she offered. "He demands that you come to him to meet first. In his setting and context, as it were. Possibly, for you to understand him better, but I'm willing to bet that he wishes to score some points on his associates by showing that he really does have a mission, a grant, and financial backing."

She closed the file and handed it across the desk.

"All the information you need is in here, and electronic copies will be transmitted to *Marrakesh* with more research and background material added after we've been able to filter from the space vampires bits," she said. "You'll be meeting him *in situ*, as it were, three days from today."

"Uniformed?" Padraig asked sharply.

"I leave that up to you, Captain," she nodded. "Review the

files, meet the Professor, then make your arrangements to depart, knowing that we will be loading two Cargo Pods with as much food and basic gear as we can stow, to allow you to remain in the field as long as possible. There is the potential for resupply later, though if you find something truly interesting, you'll probably be joined by a full squadron and possibly a mobile base. Again, you will ascertain the needs based on the situation and inform me. Anything else?"

"Not at present, sir," he said. "I'll file a set of questions once I read the material, and possibly after I meet this man."

"Dismissed, then, Captain, Squire," she said, watching them rise. "And good luck."

Padraig nodded.

Sounded weird. But that was an improvement over fighting. His was a Tactical Transport, not a Line Cruiser.

And he had a lot of homework to do, it seemed.

2

———

Padraig had decided to dress in mufti for this...whatever it was. Basic civilian clothing, with blue slacks, white pullover shirt, and a black jacket he occasionally wore when out on an autumn day off duty on some planet.

He wasn't armed, but he had sent Lead Expert Cameron Farrell ahead, his senior security crew member from *Marrakesh*. And she hadn't transmitted any message to abort the meeting, so Padraig was crossing the landing lot and approaching the front door.

Night Eyes Brewing was the place, with a pair of animalistic eyes done in a green faded down towards yellow, pupils vertically slitted like a cat or something, on a black background. No other hints as to what kind of creature it might represent, but Padraig had spent two days deep diving into that *other world*.

He didn't want to say he might have pulled something rolling his own eyes at some of these peoples' beliefs, but he didn't want to lie either. Some folks apparently needed something to believe in, and not all of them fell into any of the various organized religions out there.

Or maybe cryptozoology was its own religion? Hard to tell. Stories of the ancient Spider Goddess whose hyperspace webs originally linked all worlds. Or the Intergalactic Plasma Space Dragons who laid eggs on various worlds in the form of an *Aurora* or *Australia Borealis*. The supposed godlike being that lived at the exact center of the galaxy, watching everyone and everything. Tentacles in space that appeared and captured starships, making them vanish entirely.

Padraig had spent too many years in the hard confines of the military, with all its emphasis on realism, to wander off on such flights of fancy, but he supposed that he was a bad judge of what people needed emotionally.

He entered the bar, unsurprised that the lights were set dimmer than usual. And no sportsball events on any of the video screens. Instead, old movies, with the main one showing some sort of monstrous flying creature in the process of destroying a city on some world, though the sound was turned down.

Cameron Farrell was at the bar, ignoring some of the folks sitting near her to concentrate on a beer and watch the room in the bar mirror. She was armed. And extremely dangerous. He felt safer already.

Padraig moved to an empty table and climbed up onto a stool, though he could have just as easily stood at it. A waiter appeared from somewhere, putting a glass of water and a menu in front of him.

"Get you anything?" the man asked.

Padraig paused to study the man, but couldn't identify the costume or maybe uniform he was wearing. Looked vaguely military, with crimson with strange tags and patches.

"Coffee," Padraig decided.

Beer might be nice, but he had no idea what Professor Whitlaw would be like, other than an academic exiled from *Wronlori* who had somehow made it this far, then existed in *A'Zedi* space despite the two nations being at war again. Or still.

The waiter nodded and departed.

A man detached himself from a nearby table and walked

closer. Farrell locked onto him, but Padraig didn't think the man noticed.

Dressed in cheap pants and jacket. And not the Professor. Too young, for one thing. And weirdly proportioned, like a stick figure that had stepped out of the screen, with a build like a toothpick someone had stuck a grape onto. Weird eyes.

Probably make one hell of a good character actor if he wanted, since he had serious *That Guy* vibes going on, but the man smiled as he got close.

"Stranger?" the man asked.

"Meeting someone," Padraig replied in a friendly tone.

"Oh?" the stranger asked. "Who?"

Padraig studied the man but didn't sense any serious hostility. And Farrell could be on him in about four steps if she felt the need.

"Professor Whitlaw," Padraig said simply, watching for a reaction. Any reaction.

He wasn't prepared for the scowl. Farrell's head came up just a bit out of the corner of his eye.

"You from the government?" the man asked.

"Vaguely," Padraig admitted, without admitting anything. "Part of the grant."

Also truth. Technically correct was the best kind of correct, after all.

"Need crew?" the man asked, taking a step forward and holding out a hand. "Gary Renshaw."

Padraig wasn't prepared for the man to suddenly turn friendly, but he shook with the man, noting the callouses from a lot of hard work with one's hands.

"Got crew," Padraig started to say, when an angry voice echoing across the space cut him off.

"Renshaw, you leave him alone," the man snarled.

Padraig let go as Renshaw stepped back sharply and turned to the newcomer.

Professor Nicodemus Whitlaw. Tall and lean, like a hawk in

many ways. Bald, with a rich goatee in salt and pepper. Pale, like the folks from *Wronlori* tended to be, instead of the darker browns of *A'Zedi*. Dressed in a functional gray jumpsuit with a lot of pockets and a black shirt visible at the neck. Sharp blue eyes, which were so rare around here.

"What are you about, Renshaw?" Whitlaw demanded as he stepped close.

From somewhere, the waiter had managed to slip in and deliver coffee, but Padraig had missed it, focused elsewhere until he noted the mug.

"Nothing," Renshaw replied. "Asking about work."

"And what would you know about work, Renshaw?" the Professor asked archly.

Padraig leaned back with the mug in one hand and watched, wondering if he should get involved or not. Especially when Renshaw recoiled as if struck with a physical blow.

"It's not fair, Professor," Renshaw said sourly. "You got a grant. Money. You get to go look. I'm stuck here on UBI and day work. I'll never manage to find them."

Padraig didn't ask who *they* were, but watched Renshaw slink off without another word. The Professor watched triumphantly, then turned back this way.

"Boru?" he confirmed.

"That's right, Professor," Padraig replied. "Your friend was inquiring about crew work, but I told him that I had crew and to talk to you about billets instead. Man has rough hands."

"We all scramble to survive, Boru," Whitlaw said, taking the stool across the table.

The waiter returned with a beer and a shot glass filled with something clear, then disappeared without a word, so Padraig assumed that the Professor was indeed a regular. And he did have legitimate funds right now to perhaps celebrate and enjoy himself a bit.

Others besides Renshaw might sniff around, but *Marrakesh* had secrets that needed to be kept.

"So what questions can I answer for you, Professor?" Padraig asked. "I was told you wanted to meet here first and foremost, before loading up and moving out."

Whitlaw studied him long and hard.

"Patriot?" Whitlaw asked.

"That's right," Padraig agreed. "Sailor doing a job in a war I didn't ask for."

"Nor I, Boru," he said. "The *United Technocracy* doesn't forbid research into exoarchaeology, but it was a good way to make enemies. They like to think that they invented their entire civilization from whole cloth. Lifted themselves up from nothing, without admitting that *A'Zedi* really did manage that, while *Wronlori* largely inherited the industrial core of the old *Riffrost* worlds and built up from there."

Padraig nodded. Most of this had been distilled in the briefing packet, and he had Nyssa Taggart diving deep into all sorts of things that Padraig barely had the security clearance to know.

"So what's out there, Professor?" Padraig prompted, mostly to see how much matched with what he'd read.

"A world that has old ships on it," Whitlaw said. "The linguistic drift is sufficient that I cannot be certain whether it was a junkyard, a scrapyard, a boneyard, or merely a singular wreck. Merely that later explorers reported finding one or more ships on this world, then filed their data. The information was then lost for several centuries. I applied for a grant, like I usually do, but I was utterly astonished that it was approved."

Padraig nodded. As had the Permanent First Secretary been surprised. And him.

"Somebody saw something in your grant that they liked," Padraig told him. "And decided that you needed better resources than just that grant to actually go investigate it. Especially as far away as it purports to be. We'll be loaded to the gills and still living lean. I need you to tell me if what you find when get there is valuable enough to do something unconventional like assign you as planetary governor and ask my superiors for help."

"You'd do that?" Whitlaw gasped, so utterly shocked that he almost spilled his beer down his front.

"I'm your transport, sir," Padraig replied, threading a fine legal needle between the grant language and his orders from Gelashvili. "I am not an expert on exoarchaeology. Nor is anyone on my crew. That's you and yours."

Whitlaw digested that, his eyes still filled with a bit of disbelief.

"How soon could you depart?" he finally asked.

"We're ready to load," Padraig replied. "I need a count of people you'll take with you so we can calculate consumables. Also, a volume of gear to load."

Whitlaw got cagey at that.

"There might be a slight difficulty," he said, cringing like Padraig might tear up the contract right there and then.

"That being?" Padraig asked carefully.

It wasn't his decision to make, but he could always raise a fuss with his bosses if necessary.

"I was able to acquire a small orbital shuttle after the funds were confirmed," he said. "The grant had funds for equipment such as that. It's in flyable condition, though it might need some work. It has a complete laboratory that I can use in the field to clean and identify any artifacts we discover, as well as some other gear I might find useful."

Padraig did the math. Small suggested a class down from *Roadrunner* or *Flight of Fancy*, which were both medium-lifter hulls.

"How big?" he asked, listening as Whitlaw laid out the dimensions and mass.

Yup, small. Barely larger than most ground vehicles.

"We should be able to load it, though it won't fly without rearranging my flight bay," Padraig said. Gelashvili had told him to make things happen. That involved odd things like this, he supposed. "Where did you get it?"

"It is a retired mobile police crime lab," Whitlaw offered, grinning wryly. "Useful to be transported on most small freighters, such as I was initially expecting. Or to be assigned to a single world where it could fly to any location and operate autonomously."

"Anything else?" Padraig asked. "Big things?"

"I don't really have a digging crew," Whitlaw said. "And I'm not sure if the grant stretches to allow me to hire your crew members to operate in the field."

Padraig paused and processed that. Strong backs and sharp minds were necessary when committing archaeology, from what he'd read. Dig away top layers of soil with picks and shovels, then move more delicately to get to every artifact. Or even discolorations in the soil where something buried had rotted away, leaving little.

"I intend to assign a few folks to the ground mission," he offered. "Support and security mostly, so they can cook and make sure the local fauna doesn't threaten you, but I don't have any experts."

"I can train someone in a matter of days," Whitlaw said with the wave of a hand. "And we won't know what we're facing until we get there."

"The grant has space for ten people, including yourself," Padraig offered. "Have you talked to the local universities?"

"I have not." Whitlaw turned frosty. "They would steal my find and my glory if I let them."

"You have several days before I'm ready to depart, Professor," Padraig said, turning hard himself. "Hopefully, you will be able to recruit some staff."

"I have four now with myself," Whitlaw said. "Ten, you say?"

Padraig nodded.

"Six more berthing spaces have been reserved," Padraig confirmed. "Anyone joining you will be subject to a basic background check, but my understanding is that such a review is for open warrants, rather than socially questionable ideas."

A delicate way to say that goofballs and borderline nut cases were acceptable, but not punks and thieves.

And Gelashvili had already provided him some reports of folks associated with the crowd that drank at the *Night Eyes Brewing*. Weirdos, but nothing that dangerous, as far as he could tell.

Save for one exiled *Wronlori* academic.

"I will need to make inquiries," Whitlaw said.

"Good," Padraig replied. "And we need to go over some of the details about your transportation. Meanwhile, what can you suggest for our meal? The government is buying."

3

Commander Chance Messier sat in her office, thinking about the various departments and divisions as she read the latest weekly reports. Just outside, Padraig had command on the bridge.

She liked to say that she'd done a little bit of everything in her time. When she'd confirmed that she was pregnant with Xandra, she'd been put on shore duty. There hadn't been a war going on at the time, so she hadn't been certain there would be billets open when she was ready to return, especially not after she had had Daneel two years later. Instead, she'd made it a point to cycle through as many lateral options and training programs as she could manage in her spare time, with Robin happy being a house-husband even before then and carrying more than half the load.

Human Resources. Intelligence Analysis. Survey Corps. Electronics Engineering. Hell, she'd even qualified as an Emergency Medical Technician in her spare time.

Anything to get her back into space when she could do so.

Then *Wronlori* had attacked Eworn, and the Fleet had reactivated every hull and warm body they could lay hands on, promoting her to Commander and assigning her as First Officer aboard *Marrakesh*.

Hell of a way to win at life.

She had not, to date, spent any time in exoarchaeology—the study of human activities in a space environment—there having been no alien life more advanced than certain lichens identified anywhere to date.

But Whitlaw had proven to be pretty good at explaining the basics to people. And couldn't go much past that, because nobody knew if they'd find a ship sitting abandoned on a landing field, buried halfway, or scattered in pieces either accidentally or from being parted out over time.

Still, she'd read everything on Taggart's new reading list. And spent time talking to Whitlaw and his people once they'd loaded and *Marrakesh* had gotten in motion.

Apparently, Gary Renshaw had been a late addition that Padraig had found surprising, but the mousy guy had largely kept to himself, beyond some flirting with female crew members. None of them, however, had been all that impressed with the man.

Chance certainly wasn't, even if she would have been single. Weird vibes. Weird eyes. Weird everything.

Her comm chimed.

"First Officer," Chance said.

"Flight Deck. Rafferty," the Air Boss replied. "Got an interesting request here and need an officer to figure out which interference to run. Has to do with the *Crime Lab*."

That was how the crew had taken to describing the little lifter shuttle wedged back in a corner of the flight bay, a kitten next to Rafferty's other two big cats.

"Something you can file?" she asked the man.

"I'd kinda prefer to handle this one verbally, sir," Rafferty replied. "If possible."

"I'll be there in five," she replied.

"Thank you," and he cut the line.

Chance flipped a coin in her head and decided to swing by the forward cargo bay on her way aft. She found Kaitlin in her small office that was just barely big enough for a chair and a horizontal surface to work on.

"What's up?" the Stevedore asked as Chance came to the doorway.

"Air Boss wants help with the *Crime Lab*, but wants it kept quiet," Chance replied. "Wondered if you were bored enough to come with."

"Other than someone has to keep folks from pilfering the good stuff out of these boxes when nobody is looking, I've got almost nothing to do," Kaitlin laughed, rising. "Anything to keep me sane."

Chance laughed, too, as they fell in and headed aft.

"How's the guest portion of things going?" she asked.

"Whitlaw is used to ships," Kaitlin acknowledged. "He's been no trouble. Some of the others have barely traveled between worlds and it shows. Renshaw apparently nearly swallowed his tongue when he realized that *Marrakesh* was a Tactical Transport."

"Any troubles from the man?" Chance asked sharply.

Crew morale was her job, until something rose to the level where Padraig had to get involved.

"None as yet, but I have folks watching all of them," Kaitlin nodded. "Three women and six men including Whitlaw. He couldn't fill that last slot?"

"Fifty/fifty he didn't trust enough people to actually bring them versus he gets a cabin to himself this way," Chance laughed.

Kaitlin grinned.

"There is that."

They got to the flight deck and found Rafferty standing in the corner of the bay with Rod Garber, the Ship's Carpenter, and Expert Sailor Yua Kaneko, one of Garber's engineers.

Kaneko was a small woman, as tiny as Garber was big. As lean and smooth as Garber was a bit rough-hewn. Both mechanical nerds of the first order.

"What have you got for me?" Chance asked, looking at the group.

They were alone, but Rafferty owned this space and ran a tight ship.

"A request from the Professor to inspect the *Crime Lab* and maybe handle some basic maintenance under terms of funding from the grant," Garber began. "I looked, and the contract covers easy shit, like changing filters and filling fuel and fluids."

Chance nodded and waited. They'd asked her here for a reason. And everyone had taken to calling him *The Professor* in conversation.

"Problem is, sir, that thing needs more," Kaneko spoke up. "Like a full engine overhaul. Maybe someone taking apart life support and cleaning everything before putting it back together. Thing's almost as old as *Marrakesh*, but not nearly as loved."

Ah. That was it.

"And you'd like to handle all that under the guise of Whitlaw's original request anyway?" she asked, looking from one face to the next.

"Crew training, if nothing else," Rod Garber nodded. "New equipment. New certifications. Crap like that. But I don't know how the Professor will react. Nor the Captain. Kinda coloring outside the lines here."

"And we'll likely have crew aboard that vessel when it lands," Chance reminded him. "Plus, we are supposed to ensure the safety of our passengers. How much work are we talking?"

"Won't know until I get in there and pull things apart, sir," Kaneko nodded. "Looks like crap. Like they bought it at a police auction."

"Actually, they bought it out of the police motor pool, where it had been functionally abandoned," Kaitlin interjected with a chuckle. "And managed to fly it to orbit to dock with us. I agree that it is currently in pretty poor shape and I'm not sure I'd ride it down to any planetary surface as is."

Change considered her words.

"You go ahead and get it flightworthy," she ordered Rafferty. "Using whatever ship resources are necessary to meet Fleet requirements. Since we're transporting it, I can justify it as an *A'Zedi* military shuttle, so your butts are covered. And I'll talk to the Professor."

"Chance, why don't I handle that?" Kaitlin interjected.

"You sure?"

"Technically, he's part of the Cargo Pod assignment," she nodded. "Even if they're bunking shipside. So that falls under Stevedore, and I might have been slacking a bit on that, because some of those folks are a little weird."

"Only some?" Garber asked.

"I don't know all of them yet," Kaitlin clarified. "Leaving space to be wrong."

"I'll leave that part in your hands," Chance said, then turned back to the others. "You three need me for anything else?"

"Nope," Rafferty nodded. "As long as we have official cover, we can get that thing knocked into shape."

"You do that," Chance told them. "Kaitlin, let me know how it goes with the Professor. I'm going to let Padraig know what we're up to, but quietly."

They all nodded, then split into their functions and she left them to their business.

First Officer covered a lot of sins, but she was a big girl. She could handle them.

4

Kaitlin approached the hatch. Whitlaw had taken the last cabin on the left, at the end of the corridor, presumably so that folks making noise outside weren't at his hatch when they did.

She rang the buzzer and waited.

About the time she was ready to ring it again, the hatch slid sideways.

Kaitlin was a compact woman, so she was looking up at him as he focused on her from his great height.

Probably didn't understand how quickly she could have his ass on the deck and tied into square knots if she had to. He was an intellectual, after all.

"Is there a problem, Stevedore Lynch?" he asked after a breath to rearrange whatever he'd been about to say when he arrived.

"A request, Professor," she countered. "Perhaps we could talk privately?"

A growl appeared in his eyes, but she got that. the man was an exile, and had been hunted by the authorities back home. Then tolerated in the land of possibly his worst enemies growing up.

Privacy, and she was asking to invade it.

"We can retire to my office," Kaitlin offered when he paused.

"No, this is fine," Whitlaw said. "Come in."

He stepped back and she followed.

Standard crew cabin. Bunk bed with two closets built in and both a chair and a small desk. Officers had the same volume, save for Padraig and Chance, without having to share.

Kaitlin glanced at the desk and saw a paper notebook open with a few books handy and a reader, so she moved diagonally to the chair to sit, getting as far away from his secrets as she could with the hatch closed.

She didn't need to know.

By the time she sat, the notebook was covered. She wasn't surprised.

"There is a problem with the cargo?" he asked her, turning his seat at the desk around after detaching it from the deck.

"Not precisely," Kaitlin replied. "You had asked Air Boss Rafferty to investigate doing some maintenance on your shuttle. They have looked, but determined that more work might be necessary."

She paused there, mostly to see how he would react. When *Marrakesh* was hauling pods, they usually came with an attached crew, and a good portion of her job was working with any newcomers to learn how *Marrakesh* and Padraig Boru operated. Smooth over troubles and personality issues.

Whitlaw was an emotionally contained man, but she presumed that exile had made him careful about opening himself up.

"How much?" he asked in a tone wondering if someone was about to pull the rug out from under his feet.

How many such rugs had he known in his time? Probably many.

"I've talked with some folks, and they'd like your permission to use the shuttle as a training facility for the engineering crew," she offered, turning his mind sideways with her words. "It is a piece of gear they don't know, so folks can learn new systems. Earn new certifications that might prove useful later. And fix it up better in the process."

He started to talk three times, closing his mouth each time and rethinking.

"I don't understand," he finally admitted.

"We're going to go ahead and do all the work right now," she explained.

"But why?" he asked. "And I cannot afford that. I could barely afford the shuttle as it was. And I had few other needs, so it represented the bulk of my expenses charged to the grant."

Kaitlin nodded.

Academic, then and now. Used to minuscule budgets and excessive bureaucracy, because academia frequently had smart, bored people offered the tiniest bit of power, to the point that it drove many of them mad.

Marrakesh spent more on quarterly maintenance supplies alone.

"Captain Boru wants your mission to succeed, Professor," Kaitlin explained calmly. "Sometimes, that means the crew have to go a bit above and beyond their normal duties. This is one of those times. Knowing the people involved, they intend to get the shuttle as close to new as possible. Partly, they expect to be using that craft later, and want it to be safe. Partly, we're talking about their professional pride, which is a thing I am certain you understand."

She left it at that, watching her words puff the man up a bit.

Ego was a terrible taskmaster, but it could be harnessed.

He started to speak and caught himself.

"You can speak," she said. "As Stevedore, I am frequently called on to keep secrets from the rest of the crew, mostly because I have to work with transported passengers and some of their lives don't need to be known to the crew."

He studied her closely, those bright blue eyes like a hawk's, as Padraig had mentioned.

So pale, compared to most of the folks she knew. And most of this crew.

"The *United Technocracy* does not operate like this, Stevedore Lynch," he finally admitted.

Kaitlin nodded.

"*Wronlori* is all about automation," she acknowledged. "I get that. Machines to do as much work as possible. People to make sure the machines work, but maybe not given much attention themselves. *Marrakesh* has a proud crew, in spite of being an old boat pressed into service because of the war with your old countrymen. They are offering to extend that pride to you and yours. Personally, I'd take them up on it, because I know these people. I know how hard they will work to overcome every challenge it throws at them. Possibly because of that."

He blinked rapidly, silently, confusedly.

"Why?" he whispered.

Kaitlin smiled warmly.

"Because you're offering them something special, Professor," she said.

"But it's just an old junker shuttle," he replied, still lost.

"Not that," she shook her head. "You're offering this crew an *adventure*. To go to some world that maybe nobody has visited in centuries. To see lost sights. To maybe find an old starship that they can repair and fly away. Something hundreds or even thousands of years old that they can walk on. Touch. Know. What kid didn't dream of that?"

He nodded, licking his lips as his brain processed all that.

She could almost watch his mind break into several large pieces, then rearrange itself into a new format, but Kaitlin was pretty good at this side of things.

Her job was as much den mother as referee and translator.

"You approve, I take it?" she asked, rising and towering a bit over the seated man.

"Yes," he whispered. "And thank them for me."

"Oh, I'll let you do that, Professor," she smiled as she moved to the hatch. "They'll want to show off to you when they're done."

"Okay," he managed, staggering to his feet. "My pardon, it is just a difficult thing for me to understand."

"I know, Professor," she said, sliding into the corridor. "But it's who we are."

She nodded as the hatch slid closed in his face.

He'd come around.

5

Nyssa had two jobs as Radio Officer. Well, three, but there wasn't anybody around for her to indulge in her job as cryptographic spy, so she was concentrating on communications and sensors.

Marrakesh was in no great hurry, so they were generally racing along at the sedate speed of Mark Three. Three light-years per hour, though not in a straight line because they needed to shift around stars and system as they went.

Specifically, they had to skirt the edges of the *Enlightened Tyranny of Traisa* claimed space on their starboard side, while not getting close to *Wronlori* to port. Some sneaking, but mostly just plotting a winding course to stay outside of the range where anybody's Aetherial Sensors could see them.

They would still be more than three weeks in flight getting there.

Captain had convinced the Professor to provide the rough coordinates they needed early on. It would get them to within fifteen or so light-years, if she had to guess, based on starlogs so ancient that she felt a little queasy just thinking about them.

Hadn't anybody ever done a proper survey?

Nyssa must have made a sound, because Captain Boru spoke up and interrupted her train of thought.

"What was that, Radio?" he asked.

Nyssa shook her head and turned to look at him. Captain's face invited a comment, so she drew a breath.

"Lack of proper surveys of the region in question, sir," she said. "Why hasn't anybody done one more recently?"

He nodded and turned thoughtful.

"Because we're currently in the middle of the War of the Fourth Alliance, Squire," he said soberly. "*Wronlori* and *A'Zedi* have been at war—hot, cold, or luke warm—for better than a century, with *Traisa* sometimes on our side, sometimes theirs, and sometimes neutral, as today. Same with the *Holy Imperium of Copez*. Organized surveys are expensive, because you have to have a lot of ships, and resupply them regularly."

"Oh," she nodded. "That makes sense."

"Plus, there's a lot of entropy involved," he continued before she could turn back to her boards.

"Sir?"

"Status quo is a beguiling thing, Taggart," he nodded back. "On top of that, I'm reasonably certain that there are colony worlds out there that don't want to talk to anybody from the more central regions. Maybe religious isolationists. Maybe pirates. Maybe they just don't like people. Either way, not our problem."

"Pirates?" she asked, glancing sideways at where Maddox Nevin—Ship's Gunner—sat.

"I got you covered, Radio," Maddox said quietly. "You find them. I'll crush them."

"I'm hoping that's not necessary, Gunner," Captain called.

"You and me both, sir," Maddox turned back and nodded. "Still, it's my job to be prepared for it if it has to happen."

"Indeed, Armiger," Captain replied. "Taggart, remember that you're the survey officer that will file all these new reports when we get back."

"Do we want our names attached, sir?" she asked him, harking back to the fact that *Marrakesh* was technically a spy ship these days, and a number of crew in on the things they were doing for Intelligence Operations.

"Not our call, Radio," Captain Boru nodded. "Most of those records will only be for the Fleet anyway. I presume that there is a significant lag before they are added to the general sailing directions that get published for civilians."

Nyssa paused to consider that, then turned and started typing. She had access to some amazingly powerful datacores that had been added during the overhaul that turned *Marrakesh* from a mere Tactical Transport into an intelligence ship. Stupendous amounts of data, awaiting her needs to be turned into information.

She found the answer quickly.

"Thirty years from discovery seems to be the standard, sir," Nyssa told the Bridge. "Presumably the senior officers involved will be fully retired at that point, and any younger crew likely at the end of their careers?"

"Just so, Taggart," he said with a laugh. "You'll be an ancient woman of fifty-one by then."

Nyssa laughed with him. She was still the youngest officer on the ship, though there would be new graduates from the Academy in another year or two that would be her age.

She'd enlisted at seventeen to escape home. Then been tested by sharp folks and offered more and more options as they discovered that she was a lot smarter than she'd let on in school once she discovered how ostracized the bright kids could be. Twenty-one now. Squire soon to be promoted to Armiger, perhaps. Radio Officer.

And spy.

"Fleet Marshall Taggart?" she asked him.

"I can't see any reason why you couldn't, Nyssa," he nodded.

Her? Fleet Marshall? Highest military rank available, below only the Grand Marshall, who was the civilian-appointed head of the Fleet?

Heady thoughts. Frightening, even.

And they were sailing into darkness here, so she might still be in uniform when records of this mission came out, though Nyssa suspected that *A'Zedi* Intelligence Operations probably would file off all those serial numbers before declassifying these records. Or marking them Top Secret until the youngest crew member involved was dead.

Hidden for a century? Maybe safer, with some of the things they'd done before now.

Nyssa nodded to acknowledge the Captain's words, then went back to her scans, refining the forward array a bit more and tuning things.

If Professor Whitlaw's mission was successful enough, there might be many more *A'Zedi* ships headed this direction.

They would need to know the best way to sail it.

That was her job.

6

———————

Padraig looked up as his door chime chirped. He was in his main office, away from the bridge, doing paperwork, so the break was probably more welcome than he was willing to admit.

He opened it to Armiger Nevin.

"Am I interrupting, sir?" Maddox asked.

"Negative, sailor," Padraig smiled. "I need a break. Come in and sit. What's on your mind?"

Padraig always felt that he'd been trained up by some of the best officers possible, and strove to both emulate them and train his own officers and crew the same way. Part of that involved keeping an open door policy that let people bring him issues directly if they felt they were big enough.

Maddox was focused, but not nervous.

"Thinking about your conversation with Taggart yesterday, sir," he began. "The survey part of what we're doing, over and above the things we don't talk about with outsiders."

Padraig nodded. By now, most of his crew understood that they'd moved beyond the sorts of things an old tug like *Marrakesh* should normally be involved with.

"We're sailing places no *A'Zedi* vessel has gone in a long time," Padraig agreed. "Perhaps ever. There are old records, but as she

35

noted, they are ancient, so we have to update them. What concern draws you to my door?"

"Thinking about my future career, Captain," Maddox answered. "Dunno about Fleet Marshal, but not certain where I'm likely to go next. Or when."

Padraig nodded. He'd had that exact conversation with the First Secretary. Of all his officers, Maddox Nevin was likely to be the first one he lost, when the Armiger was ready to be promoted to Knight. Maybe to a First Officer slot on a frigate somewhere, if not getting his own command of a smaller corvette.

"A lot of that is up to you, Maddox," Padraig offered. "I've had conversations with my bosses and they'd like to keep as much of this crew together as long as possible. Your name came up."

"Mine, sir?" he asked, maybe a bit surprised, but Maddox was still young.

He hadn't really internalized what Padraig and Nyssa were up to, other than to take his job as Gunnery Officer that much more seriously, training and preparing for any combat situation that might break out because they were more likely to see such trouble than most vessels.

"Yours, Nevin," Padraig confirmed. "I understand that where you might want to go next in your career might take you away from us. And I'll support your decision one hundred percent, because you're a good officer and you'll make an excellent First Officer somewhere, then Captain someday."

Maddox leaned back in his chair, eyes huge with surprise, blinking too rapidly.

"My question for you, Armiger," Padraig offered into that vast silence. "You know that *Marrakesh* is no longer operating primarily as a support vessel, correct?"

He waited for Maddox to nod before proceeding.

"There are a variety of secondary roles that don't involve Line ships," Padraig continued. "*Marrakesh* operates in the shadows, like *Northwind* who we recently rescued. Survey Corps almost always has open billets because a lot of folks would rather be on the front line, where they think the glory is. And it might be, to a certain degree, but the warfighters still need the folks that deliver fresh cream and new socks in order to succeed. That's Transport Command, which is technically us, at least on paper, though you are aware that most of the time we get orders from Intelligence Operations instead. Even Construction Command needs officers, because somebody has to build, repair, and deal with getting the warfighters back on duty after a battle. You could do any of them."

"Any, sir?" Maddox asked in a whisper.

"You are poised at that point in your career, Gunner," Padraig nodded. "Your next promotion likely sets you on a path that you will follow for the rest of your time in uniform, but you have options. Plus, the powers-that-be do like us, so they'll probably look with favor on anything you want to pursue. I'm assuming you intend to remain in uniform?"

It was always useful to confirm these things. Maddox had also been in the Navy long enough that a next service contract might not be intended, though Padraig had no reason to not want him.

"Survey Corps has slots, sir?" Maddox asked. "Senior ones?"

Padraig smiled.

"Lots of folks want to fight, not just sail, Maddox," he replied. "I went from Knight to Commander to Captain in three months, because they needed officers to fill out the bulk of support vessels and I could bring *Marrakesh* online. Otherwise, I might be a Commander and First Officer on a Line cruiser somewhere. Or maybe commanding a Frigate while still waiting for my fifth ring."

"Survey Corps ever fight?" Maddox asked, face screwed into confusion.

"Let you in on a little secret, Nevin?"

"Sir, yes, sir."

"They probably fight more than Line Command does," Padraig smiled. "They just don't talk about it as much. Pirates and folks like that might not want someone knowing where they are operating. Or where they have hidden their base. They'll jump a

Survey vessel and try to capture or destroy it to protect their secrets. Maybe they don't get into as many tangles as we have on *Marrakesh*, but they generally see more fighting than most Line vessels do, because those ships mostly protect planets and bases from attacks, then occasionally go attack others."

"Huh," Maddox grunted. "So that might be a way to get ahead? A leg up if I did want to come back to Line later?"

"You already have more direct combat experience than most Gunnery Officers I know, Maddox," Padraig nodded. "With your background, I could see them putting you in command of a Patrol Corvette on surveys. The kind where you'd be out hunting after pirates, and either smashing them yourself or vectoring down the big ships to crush some pirate base. But you don't have to decide today. We'll be out for several months on this mission, assuming everything goes anywhere close to plan. Then time back home for recuperation. Take six months, then we'll have a more serious conversation, but do not hesitate to come and ask me questions. Or Commander Messier, because she's kinda done everything at this point. She'll probably have some useful pointers I wouldn't think of."

"Thank you, Captain," Maddox said, rising and much more confident than when he'd walked in. "You've given me a lot to think about."

"You'll make the right decision, Gunner," Padraig told him. "And I'll support you."

Then he was alone, deep in thought. Certainly, he would lose Maddox Nevin at some point. Nature of the beast in naval service. The others would stay longer, but that just meant that he'd train them all up for their next commanding officers. Or the next crews they ended up commanding.

Part of the life of a Captain, even in the middle of a war.

7

Nyssa reviewed the records that Intelligence Operations had sent along, comparing them to what little Professor Whitlaw had let her see of his own. She hadn't bothered explaining to the man that she could dissect any datacore he might own. She also hadn't tried.

For now, she had a sphere roughly fourteen light-years across, with six stars in it all marked as interesting in the sailing directions. Only problem was that none of these records were younger than her father.

Fifty-something years since any *A'Zedi* or allied vessel had passed through here. She doubted that it was empty. Nyssa was certain that folks just didn't let those records get back home to Horwin. Maybe they knew more in *Wronlori* space. Or on Zuluo, the capital world of the *Enlightened Tyranny of Traisa*, where Supreme Autocrat Arodd Torray held power today.

Nothing she could access.

At the same time, *Traisa* and *Wronlori* didn't trade much, even with *Traisa* neutral in the current war, so there didn't appear to be much shipping traffic running across these regions of space.

Quiet, which made sense, because otherwise someone would

have likely discovered whatever the Professor had found and come to investigate it.

Assuming they hadn't already, which nobody would know until they got close. Right now, all she had was a collection of *old* sailing records and light from stars moving at its own speed through space.

Then she had an idea.

Nyssa turned to where Commander Messier had command on the bridge right now, instead of aft on the Secondary Bridge.

"You have something, Taggart?" Messier asked when Nyssa's bald head came around to look.

"Thinking survey thoughts, sir," Nyssa admitted.

"Go on."

"We don't know much about these worlds, save what someone wrote down decades or even centuries ago," Nyssa nodded. "Would it be worth dropping out of Ghost-space to point our sensors at some of these systems to see if we could pick up signals? Right now, we're going to just appear somewhere at our destination and look around, with no idea who or what might be there."

"Any suspicions?" Messier asked.

"Mostly the semi-obsessive need to update all my records, sir," Nyssa admitted. "To see if any of these worlds are broadcasting any regular signals that we might miss, blasting by at high speed."

"How long would you need?" Messier asked. "And how many times should we drop out?"

Nyssa goggled at her superior. It had been more of a lark than anything, but Commander Messier seemed to be taking it seriously. Maybe she should, too?

"I can program the sensors to do a wide spectrum pull, sir," Nyssa said, mind already racing ahead. "If we dropped out for about an hour at several places, we'd have a lot more astronautical and signals data that we could process and review later. Half a dozen, maybe up to ten, depending on how much detail you want to gather. It slows our arrival by a half-day or so, but I am not aware that we're on any particular schedule?"

"We are not," Messier nodded. "And I think updating all our records is a good thing."

Nyssa watched Messier turn to Doolan Ennis, sitting next to Nyssa in the Helm chair.

"Ennis, you work with Radio to find interesting crossroads to settle into and listen," Messier ordered. "Then log my orders for Squire Halloran when she comes on duty, plus the rest of the Helm department. I'll update the Captain."

"Understood, sir," Doolan replied, turning to look at Nyssa expectantly.

Crossroads. What an interesting turn of phrase. Suddenly, Nyssa saw the map in front of her in an entirely different way.

She nodded to Ennis.

"I need a bit to organize my plans, sailor," she told him. "Look at the forward sensor cone on our current path and find me a place. I seem to remember there's a spot coming up with several bright stars all relatively close together where we can take our first look."

"Aye, sir," Ennis replied, turning to study his own boards with greater intensity.

A quiet man. Several years older than her, but only an enlisted crew member, so Nyssa had to act like an officer.

And see what she might find at one of these crossroads.

8

———

Padraig had reviewed the schedule and made it a point to be on duty at the second to last drop-point Taggart had plotted. Up until now, all of the spots she'd taken to calling crossroads connected some portions of *Wronlori* to *Traisa*, even if it was just going back to when *Riffrost* was still a singular entity, stretched across that region of space. Before *A'Zedi* even got all that organized.

Here, they'd moved beyond the lines that even the most ambitious stellar cartographers had marked as the borders of the old *United and Free Worker's Cooperative*.

Out beyond where any of their records showed anything except stars drifting in the darkness.

"Helm, what's your status?" Nyssa asked from her chair.

"Ninety seconds to drop, Radio," Zarah Halloran replied.

Padraig nodded. They'd done this seven times so far. Not found anything, but they'd never gotten less than about a half a light-year from any of the interesting places. Mostly, settled and absorbed signals that could turn into intelligence later, once the various systems had a chance to filter noise and offer interesting tidbits for Taggart and her people to review.

The main mission would still be there tomorrow.

"Taggart, show me the larger map on the main screen," he said suddenly, causing shoulders to flinch with surprise.

"Stand by, sir," Nyssa replied.

A moment later, the main screen lit up, showing a spread of stars, with two circles in purple highlighting them.

"Bottom left is our next drop, Captain," Nyssa continued. "Top right is where the Professor has us headed. I presume that we'll get a more accurate target after we finish this pass?"

"That is correct, Radio," Padraig nodded. "He's been a bit flustered that it is actually happening, and I haven't prodded him, but that's next."

She nodded back and turned to the screen.

"Eight systems that might be interesting within a five-light-year radius from our drop point, sir," she said. "None marked as inhabited, but all of our records for this region do not show any visits by survey vessels more recently than a century. Most of what we know at present comes from old astronomical studies."

"Has *Traisa* given any hints that they might be expanding on this frontier?" he asked her, watching her head waggle back and forth as she called up data from her records.

"Nothing shows, Captain," she replied. "*Wronlori* seems to be expanding more coreward than any other direction, not counting attacks on *A'Zedi* systems and bases."

"Disregard those," he said. "It is almost impossible to conquer an unfriendly planet, short of holding all orbital space and cutting any trade. If anything, they just want to keep us from being able to attack their worlds. I'm looking for something more like Varfelis Station and all that."

"The records that we recovered do show those pressures," she acknowledged. "However, we have blanks on this side. Not that they haven't. Merely that we don't have access to those records."

"Assume they are doing similar things in this direction when filtering your data," Padraig ordered. "We're not going looking, but I'd like to know if anyone is going to suddenly show up in orbit with us while we're at work."

Her head came around, bronze skin gleaming almost as brightly as her brown eyes.

"Should we drop a sensor probe off to that side, sir?" she asked, lips pressed together. "That might let us see anyone moving around at translight speeds outside our normal Aetherial Scanner ranges. Perhaps an extra hour warning, if nothing else."

"That hour might be the difference between extracting a crew from the surface and leaving them there, Squire," Padraig replied. "Plot me an arc to place three of them, facing *Wronlori* for now because we can deal easier with a *Traisan* ship that comes inquiring."

"On it, Captain," she said.

Then the main screen flickered as they exited Ghost-space and looked around at what they might see, here so far from home.

9

"Understood, Padraig," Kaitlin replied, cutting the line and keying a different number.

Her office in the forward cargo pod was still cramped, but that was because the crew was still working backwards through all the cargo they'd crammed into every available space on the ship itself before moving to empty either pod.

Deep space missions such as these were mostly a matter of logistics. Creating and executing a strategy to stretch food, fuel, and life support as long as possible without running into any dangerous edges, while waiting for something to happen.

"Whitlaw," the Professor answered from his own cabin.

"Good afternoon, Professor," Kaitlin said into the comm. "I've just spoken with Captain Boru and we're beginning our final run towards your target coordinates. We'll need to refine our path so we can arrive."

"Oh," he replied, a bit crestfallen. "I was just about to join some of my people for a late lunch. Should I delay?"

"Negative, Professor," she said. "It can wait a few hours, as we have a few more tasks to complete at this end. Would company be acceptable?"

She caught the pause at his end. Whitlaw wasn't anti-social so much as an introverted intellectual who didn't handle large groups well. Except that she suspected he could turn on the charm when standing at the front of the room lecturing.

As long as he could slink off-stage when he was done and find a quiet place to recover. She'd known a few folks like that.

"It would be a pleasure, Kaitlin," he said. "Though I'm not sure how the others might react."

"Let me worry about them," she said. "Aft wardroom?"

"Yes," he said.

"I shall see you there shortly," Kaitlin said, cutting the line and standing up to stretch.

Padraig had mentioned some of the more aggressive things he was planning in order to scour this region. Probes could send an Aetherial message to *Marrakesh* if they saw something, but it would be a fairly broad cone signal, so anyone in the path of the transmission who happened to be looking would see it.

At the same time, picking up those probes on the way home might show all manner of traffic that didn't set off any alarms, letting them know who might live out here. Acting like Survey Corps almost.

She approved.

Kaitlin caught up with Whitlaw just as he entered the wardroom, falling in behind him and noting three of his folks ahead of them in line.

Benton Mercer was a mousy woman who might have turned into an actress, had she greater self-confidence and perhaps a touch less of that manic pixie thing going. In that, she was more of a type than a person, but all of the ones who Whitlaw had recruited to join him had been regulars in that pub where Padraig had met the man.

Yves Harcrow was a tall man. Hulking, almost, save that he was soft and walked with a bit of a permanent limp. Highly intelligent, as long as you didn't get him to talking about the so-called Spider Goddess and Harcrow's theories about a different kind of hyperspace that worked more like subway tunnels that could instantaneously teleport you vast distances instead of moving into Ghost-space to travel at a medium-to-fast FTL.

Lastly, Gary Renshaw, who Kaitlin was given to understand spent much of his downtime in the forward lounge, nose almost pressed to the transsteel window, looking for evidence of his Surfers on the Solar Tides that he was convinced were out there, riding between stars like giants while waiting for one of the lesser civilizations to swing up and say hello.

Kaitlin wanted to shake her head at such nonsense but kept it to herself. All of them believed in something, and had dedicated their lives to investigating it. In that, those shared more in common with Whitlaw than just about any sailor on the ship.

She just had a hard time keeping a straight face when listening to some of their plans.

Past that, they were generally harmless. All smart. All sharp enough to survive on those same fringes that Whitlaw had. And all unwilling to give up their dreams to conform to something they saw as a dreary failure of life.

Living without dreams.

Harcrow sat next to her and ate quietly. Renshaw smiled and made a bit of small talk but fell silent whenever Benton Mercer started talking. A somewhat passive man, at least when surrounded by more extroverted personalities.

"What does Captain Boru expect to find, with these odd exits from Ghost-space?" Benton asked sharply, once they had all settled and started to eat. "None of them were on the original sailing plan he shared with us."

Kaitlin nodded and chewed, using that extra moment to sand off some of the rougher edges she might have used on the woman. Benton was nervous, not aggressive. It came out that way, but many people did the same thing.

"Since Professor Whitlaw is taking us all so far into unknown regions, Captain Boru has decided that we might be well served doing some basic survey work along the way," Kaitlin replied evenly. "Nobody knows what's out here, so we're pausing to look."

"Would that data be made available to researchers?" Renshaw asked quietly.

Kaitlin was taken a bit aback, because Gary normally spoke so little around the others, but she smiled.

"Let me talk to Squire Taggart, the Radio Officer," Kaitlin offered. "Most of it will be passive sensor data, and *Marrakesh* is not particularly well-equipped with that sort of sensor, but the goal, as I understand it, is to simply collect a lot of raw data and see if anything jumps out that we should investigate more fully later, or on the way home."

She left it at that, knowing that she'd need to have Nyssa filter off some of the things that the woman would collect. Or perhaps go back to the raw data pulls themselves, without suggesting what those new computers could do when the average crew member wasn't cleared to know. To say nothing of these civilians. Kaitlin could bury Renshaw in raw data that would take him years to sort through.

Gary nodded.

"Thank you," he said at barely more than a whisper. "We've sought the Surfers on the Solar Wind for so long without any luck. Any hints would be useful, as we've had very little luck in the more occupied sectors. Possibly, they don't consider us advanced enough to join them, but we might stumble across their paths here in the greater stellar wilderness."

Kaitlin kept her opinions out of her eyes as she nodded. Gary Renshaw had a particularly quiet kind of crazy, but he didn't present as any sort of threat. Even the female crew members had only reported that he mostly wanted to talk about his surfers, rather than spending his efforts to seduce them.

Or maybe he saw that conversation as a kind of seduction and none of the crew were all that interesting when they weren't interested in that topic.

Stevedore meant she saw all kinds. And this mission seemed populated with them.

"And the probes we're dropping?" Harcrow suddenly spoke up. "What purpose do they serve?"

"We're technically at war with the *United Technocracy*," Kaitlin reminded the big man. "*Wronlori* does not claim this region, even on their most ambitious maps, but Captain Boru felt it was better to have a wider buffer of protection, in case someone does head towards us. I presume that you will all be on the ground, if we have any luck at all, but wouldn't necessarily wish to be stuck there if *Marrakesh* had to withdraw because someone arrived in a proper warship, yes?"

She was watching Whitlaw's eyes. He understood that he faced prison, if not a labor camp, were he to fall back into the hands of his however-distant kith and kin. The others weren't as politically attuned to understand.

Whitlaw nodded.

"I'd rather make it to orbit and depart with *Marrakesh*," the man said sharply, his tone suggesting that he'd fight anyone and everyone for space on that last transport off the surface.

"If they don't claim this world, why do they care?" Benton asked.

Kaitlin shrugged.

"I cannot judge their behavior, mistress," she replied. "They declared war on *A'Zedi* and attacked. And have attacked this vessel on a few occasions as well. Captain Boru prefers to be safe. And for his crew and especially his passengers to also be safe. Those probes extend that safety to a wider margin for errors."

She left it at that. These three all technically worked for Whitlaw, so he could deal with them if they had complaints. Her job was interfacing back to Padraig. And Nyssa, she supposed, since it had been Nyssa's idea to do the extra survey work on the way out.

"And we'll really be there tomorrow?" Gary asked into the sudden lull. "Really?"

"Really," Kaitlin nodded. "This time tomorrow, we should be

sitting in orbit above our target, scanning the surface for Professor Whitlaw's clues and maybe the ships themselves."

That caused them all to lean back a little, eyes taking on that faraway gleam as they absorbed some of Whitlaw's dreams and wondered how their own might be brought to fruition by whatever gods might decide to smile on them next.

Kaitlin settled in to eat.

10

———

Maddox appreciated that Captain Boru was training him well over and above what a Gunner even on a normal Line Cruiser might expect, to say nothing of a Tactical Transport.

Captain had even gone so far as to have himself and Commander Messier off duty for many of the survey runs, letting Maddox split duty with Taggart, who was learning things, too.

She wasn't prepping for an independent command, though. At least not today. Maddox couldn't honestly say that about himself.

Right now, Command Expert Valeria Tindal—the ship's proper Gunner as senior enlisted in the department—was in Maddox's usual station, manning the weapons in case they were needed, while Maddox was in the Captain's cj\hair, exercising command authority.

At least both his bosses were immediately handy in the day office just off the Bridge, if Maddox needed them.

"Helm, how soon?" he asked, working on sounding calm and collected like how Captain Boru did it.

"Two minutes to arrival, sir," Zarah replied without looking back. "We're coming out off-plane for a normal arrival and a distance out, but I have seen no evidence of habitation from what Radio has detected."

Maddox nodded to Nyssa Taggart when she smiled at him. Lots of data accumulated. He presumed she'd be spending most of her time over the next week distilling it down into something interesting for the captain to review.

Right now, Maddox was in command.

He found the switch that let him address the entire ship, including both cargo pods and even the freezer in the aft wardroom. You never knew where someone might be at that moment they needed to hear something important.

"All hands, this is Armiger Nevin," he said slowly. "We are two minutes from arrival in an unknown system. Since we cannot be certain of our situation, stand by for orders."

He left it at that. Captain Boru hadn't wanted to come out hot and ready to fire, but also didn't want to pretend that this was a normal call on a boring, friendly—safe—port somewhere.

Be prepared for anything. Good enough.

He watched the clock tick down, then they dropped out of Ghost-space and looked around.

"Radio, give me a hard scan in all directions," Maddox ordered, barely beating Nyssa's hand to that switch anyway. "Helm, stand by to run if we have to. Guns, you stay loose but ready."

Everybody nodded. Right out of the Survey Corps handbook he'd taken to studying in his spare time, because Maddox found that he had a lot to learn if he decided to go that direction. He didn't know yet, but Captain Boru believed that more training made better officers, regardless of where you were assigned.

"No ships detected in orbit," Nyssa announced a few moments later. "Wavefront outbound also finds no ships. Two smaller moons, neither showing any signs of habitation."

Maddox nodded. Exactly what the sailing directions said, but those were so old as to be almost irrelevant.

Everything *Marrakesh* did now would update them for someone later.

Hopefully.

"Helm, plot and execute a standard orbital insertion," Maddox said. "Radio, keep watch in case someone is on the far side of the planet from us. Also, make sure you have a scanner pointed down as we circle."

"Aye, sir," Taggart and Halloran both replied in unison.

Maddox leaned back and watched his people work.

His people?

Right now, with the Captain and Commander Messier deliberately letting him handle things, yes.

Best to make it look good for everyone.

didn't take long to complete their first orbit.

"Radio," Nyssa called, drawing his head in her direction. "I show no signs of technological civilization below. Scanning of the surface continues at a slower pace."

Maddox nodded.

Technological civilization. Lights on the dark side. Radio signals bouncing around the atmosphere. Even artificial satellites in orbit, watching weather below or traffic above.

Exactly what Whitlaw had predicted, but Maddox knew how thin the information supporting his theories had been.

Somewhere—supposedly—someone had left a starship down there. Or a bunch of them.

Marrakesh wasn't designed to deorbit and land on the surface. Most ships frigate size and up couldn't. Hell, about half of the corvette designs he knew couldn't do that.

didn't mean it couldn't be done. There were some amazingly huge freighters designed to slowly wallow down, as much gliding on lifting surface designs as riding massive thrusters to get there and then back up later with a full load.

Expensive, and usually reserved for worlds exporting grains by the gigaton, where they still lacked the facilities to build and maintain a space elevator or were too cheap to slowly ship it to orbit and store it for the monster ships to pick up later.

"Any evidence of prior habitation visible from orbit?" he asked, knowing that to be almost impossible to actually see from up here, depending on the age of any ruins.

Still, it was Nyssa Taggart. He'd bet she'd be the one in a thousand who could do it.

He watched her head bob back and forth as she looked at her screens.

"Radio?" he asked.

"Maybe, sir?" she replied. "Based on human nature, I looked at the interfaces between land and water. This planet is sixty-five percent rocky, with some huge continents breaking up a bunch of smaller oceans. Same with inland rivers and deltas. There are three places that kind of stand out, but I don't have enough data to make a solid call."

"Helm, on the next orbital pass, make sure you fly over all three," he ordered. "Slowly if possible, and it's okay if our orbit looks drunk as you do it. Get Taggart as clear a view as you can."

"Aye, sir, driving on ice, coming up."

Maddox laughed. Zarah probably could drive a land vehicle over a sheet of ice and make it look normal.

He keyed the intercom and spoke the one line that he'd been waiting to say for days, drawing a breath and smiling as he spoke.

"All hands, we have arrived," he announced. "Welcome to Sabahattin."

11

———

Padraig studied the maps Nyssa had presented on the Bridge's main screen, the planet peeled like an orange and projected with distortion so it was a wide, flat rectangle.

Both poles were ice-covered, sometimes kilometers deep, so he was less worried about what might be hidden up there. The equator was a touch hot. Shorts and a loose shirt weather. Maybe with a hat.

Not a lot of orbital inclination. Maybe four degrees but they hadn't been here long enough to nail it tighter than that. Enough that there weren't going to be much in the way of seasons. You'd have hot zones, cold zones, and everything in between generally based on your latitude.

Now, he just needed to know what kind of culture they might find if there were people down there. What temperature they'd have been comfortable with.

Because there was no technology below him that Nyssa had been able to detect.

Padraig looked over at Professor Whitlaw. The others were aft, doing whatever they needed to do to get ready to walk planetside, but he needed the main brains here.

"Thoughts?" Padraig asked the man, noting the old-fashioned notebook in one hand.

Professor Whitlaw's breathing was a bit shallow and rapid, but that was just excitement.

They were really here.

Whitlaw turned to look at him and Padraig smiled at the man, nodding.

Whitlaw nodded back and blinked a few times.

"Miss Taggart, there is a small sea facing east, roughly ten degrees north of the equator," he said, addressing Nyssa. "If the notes are correct, it should be around two hundred kilometers wide and roughly circular, where it lets out into the broader ocean."

"Got it," she said, dropping a red zone onto the map off to the left from where they were currently orbiting.

"Have you scanned it closer?" Whitlaw asked, voice rising a bit. Nervous. Excited.

"Affirmative, sir," she replied. "Stand by."

Padraig watched the map blink out and a tighter image replace it. A sea, with several smaller bays visible from up here. A single river delta pressing up against a line of hills on the north edge.

Whitlaw opened his notebook and pulled out a single piece of paper. With trembling hands, he walked over and handed it to Nyssa, who studied it, nodded, and started typing.

The Professor turned in place to address Padraig.

"A printout from the original log," he said. "An orbital image they happened to append to the original report, indicating where they had found the ship. Ships. Something. The maps were filed separately. Or lost. It has been four hundred years, so I can't be certain."

"Here," Nyssa said a moment later, zooming the map down even tighter and showing a level upland on the north side of that river.

A plateau of sorts, with smaller rivers and washes flowing

south into the larger one but feeling seasonal. Like this portion of the world was largely dry, save for passing storms.

"What's the terrain, Radio?" Padraig asked.

"Generally alpine uplands here, sir," she said. "Grass and scattered forest, but nothing impenetrable. Rolling meadows and glacially-cut river valleys, I think. Still scanning the surface to gain a better understanding of recent geological history. A bit chilly from surface temp readings, but otherwise perfectly habitable."

"Stay with those scans, but concentrate things here first," he ordered. "Helm, ahead forty percent and insert us into a geosynchronous orbit directly overhead of the point where that river drops into the bay."

"Aye, sir," Zarah replied. "Adapting orbit now. ETA four minutes."

Padraig addressed himself to Whitlaw.

"We'll need a day to scan things better, Professor," he told the man. "Given the situation, I intend to pack up one of the shuttles and use it to deliver cargo and crew to a point you select on the surface, when Taggart gets us close. We'll then establish a base camp that might move around, once we know more. Your people will go down with that first load, and we'll put *Crime Lab* next to it, with my other shuttle remaining here for anything that comes up. What questions do you have?"

"Only the most obvious," Whitlaw finally smiled. "Are we really here?"

"We have, Professor," Padraig smiled back. "Now, let's go find out what *it* means."

12

Padraig opened the hatch when the chime signaled a visitor. It was late in his day, and he was working on finishing off a major report that summed up the first third of the mission: everything about getting to Sabahattin.

"Am I intruding, sir?" Maddox asked, standing on the threshold.

"Not at all, Nevin," Padraig said, sliding his screen off to one side. "What can I do for you?"

"Sir, I'd like to volunteer for the ground mission team," Maddox replied, taking a step into Padraig's office.

"Oh?"

"Expanding my horizons, sir," Nevin nodded.

"Sit," Padraig ordered, waiting a moment. "Giving thought to your next job?"

"Aye, sir," Maddox nodded. "Not sure what or where, but this is an opportunity to learn new things. To serve in different circumstances. Plus, I'm hoping that *Marrakesh* won't need a Gunnery Officer aboard while we're committing exoarchaeology. And if we do, she's got both you and Gunner Tindal, so she should be safe."

"Any thoughts on where you'll want to go next?" Padraig

asked, making a mental note to append this entire conversation to his personal log while it was still fresh in his mind.

First Secretary Gelashvili would have a sharp interest.

"No, sir," Maddox shook his head. "At the same time, I've done some deeper research on Survey Corps, and some of those billet requisitions for commanding officers allow for Knights, rather than just Commanders. Might be an opportunity to gain command experience in the field, sir."

"It would," Padraig agreed. "And the job would be largely similar to what we've been doing on the way to Sabahattin, plus what we're expecting to do starting tomorrow."

"Is that why you and Radio made a point of dropping out of Ghost-space to do those surveys, sir?" Maddox asked.

"Partly," Padraig agreed. "Partly, it needed to be done, because no *A'Zedi* ships have come this way to do that work. Normally, a cargo carrier like us would simply record what we could from Ghost-space and call it good, but I'm also working on the presumption that Whitlaw finds something out there and the Fleet will need to send more ships later. That probably includes Survey Corps flying a pass or six through this region, however quietly, because it will turn out to be more interesting than anyone knew before this."

"Have we found anything, sir?" the young man asked.

"Not yet, but Nyssa hasn't had much time to digest the data," Padraig answered. Then he pivoted mentally. "I have talked to the Stevedore about taking command of the camp on the surface. Would you prefer to handle that, Nevin?"

He watched the man lean back in his chair and consider that for a long moment.

"Actually, sir, I'd prefer to be able to lead smaller expeditions into the wilderness," Maddox replied. "If possible, that is. I understand that the Professor will have his primary dig, but we'll need to do a closer survey on the ground. If Lynch has the base, I can be her eyes and fingers out in the field."

"Excellent idea, Armiger," Padraig nodded. "You get yourself packed up tonight and I'll send you down tomorrow with the shuttle. Yours will be a roaming mission of exploration, sp I also want you to have the Corps manual in one hand. That way, you do things like they do. If this becomes your apprenticeship, I want you to look good. Understood?"

"Aye, sir," Maddox replied. "And thank you."

"This is what a commanding officer is supposed to do, Maddox," Padraig reminded him. "Keep that in mind when you're sitting on this side of the desk. And dismissed."

Maddox rose with a smile, almost bouncing up. Then he was gone.

Padraig waited a few beats after the hatch closed, then sent Kaitlin a message, updating her. Not a major change, but it would put more tools at her disposal on the surface of Sabahattin.

Who knew what they might find down there?

13

Kaitlin had taken advantage of her rank and claimed the copilot seat on *Flight of Fancy* as Teela Sanchez flew them down to the surface of Sabahattin.

More brown and gray than blue like Horwin, but still a most interesting view as they descended below the final cloud deck and saw the map stretched out below them.

Sanchez had circled west, coming in over land to let the shuttle's sensors add to what *Marrakesh* had already seen, transmitting it back to orbit in real time.

They were below five thousand meters now, cruising along below the speed of sound as they approached the bay and small sea that the Professor had identified.

"*Crime Lab*, this is *Flight of Fancy*," Sanchez said into the comm. "Coming up on our first checkpoint in thirty seconds. We'll be making a left-hand orbit twice over the target before we determine if we're landing. Copy that?"

"Roger, *Flight of Fancy*," Walt Rafferty answered from behind them in the smaller ship.

He'd pulled rank in order to fly *Crime Lab* to the surface instead of Sanchez, claiming he wanted to confirm that all the work the machine shop had done had been up to snuff, but

Kaitlin figured he just wanted to do something nobody else had. And do it first.

Sanchez would stay behind when the Air Boss flew an empty *Flight of Fancy* back to *Marrakesh*, while Walt would send someone else down with the next load of cargo. This one had just enough gear and food to survive a few days sleeping rough, while people figured out where they wanted to build something more permanent.

Kaitlin watched out the front screen as the shuttle banked left and started a wide circle.

"That it?" Sanchez asked, pointing to a spot on the near horizon.

"Those lumps, yes," Kaitlin replied. "Radio found a lot of refined metal under the dirt but couldn't get a better sense through the atmosphere. How far of a walk are you expecting?"

"Landing zone is just over a kilometer away," Teela acknowledged. "We found a spot with level ground and a large creek nearby that seems to be fed by a freshwater spring. No idea if there is anything edible in the various flora, but you'll have a good spot to work from. And folks need the exercise."

Kaitlin laughed at that.

"I'm an old woman, Teela," she replied. "Next run down you better be bringing an electric flatbed I can ride in to get to the dig."

"Talk to Walt," Teela laughed back. "I'm just flying cargo here."

Kaitlin nodded.

It was smart, setting back a bit from the dig site. And the second run would include fence posts and cyclone fencing rolls that could be strung between them to keep larger animals out. Or at least make them work at getting in, when Cam Farrell's team would be on watch keeping them out.

"*Crime Lab*, this is *Flight of Fancy*," Teela said as they completed their second pass. "I've got a spot picked out. Landing shortly, then you should have space to my east. That puts us north of the creek and on flat terrain. Landing now."

"Roger that, *Flight of Fancy*," Walt replied. "Standing by."

Kaitlin liked the way Teela shifted to lift on the thrusters and walked slowly in, almost like descending a ramp until she settled, the landing struts flexing as the weight came onto them.

Gravity on Sabahattin was about ninety percent of what Kaitlin was used to, so everything was a bit springier than normal. And she'd sleep better.

Teela got things locked down and quiet fell.

Kaitlin turned to the small mob of folks in the cargo bay, noting that both Cam Farrell and Trinh Hoàng were standing by the main airlock hatch, rather than getting ready to lower the cargo ramp.

"All yours, Cam," Kaitlin announced.

14

———

Cameron Farrell was *Marrakesh*'s only dedicated security trooper. Everyone else had other primary jobs and kept up their training on the combat and boarding side of things, including Hoàng, who worked with the Quartermaster as a supply tech.

Cameron was first through the hatch when it opened, with her Adjustable Disruptor in hand. Trinh had her Light Disruptor Cannon slung on her back, but they wouldn't have landed had there been any visible threats.

Still, Cameron's team was establishing a perimeter first and foremost. Even Armiger Nevin, nominally her boss, wasn't allowed off the shuttle until Cameron was satisfied with the situation. Overhead, *Crime Lab* was coming in, settling about forty meters away and creating the planet's first landing field of the modern age.

Cameron signaled Trinh to circle to the left while she went right. Grass underfoot. More than a mere meadow, but less than a county in size. And no straight lines over here, so natural. That was all Cameron really cared about at present.

Quickly, her dozen folks got out and into place, a ring roughly one hundred and fifty meters wide, where everyone could see the persons on each side, but were blocked from seeing across by the two shuttles.

"This is Farrell," she called. "Everything is in order?"

Voices assented and acknowledged. Calm in the mid-morning sun, according to the records Cameron had seen yesterday. Something of a chill, but she had a field shell over her normal uniform, and could dig her silks out of her bag later if it got that cold overnight. Radio had said that the temperature dropped pretty hard, but had stayed above freezing last night.

"*Flight of Fancy*, you are cleared to open your cargo bay," she said, ceding control back to Kaitlin Lynch.

Even Nevin was only along as an officer on this run, and not in charge, but Cameron had been pulled quietly aside by no less than the Captain and updated on what he had in mind for Armiger Nevin. She'd make sure that the man stayed safe, while letting him run with a lot more leash than a security marine normally allowed on the surface of a potentially hostile planet.

By standing right next to him, every time he went out.

Behind her, the whine of hydraulics as the shuttle ramp lowered. Overhead, almost no breeze. Smell of planets, which tended to be dirt and rain, when starships on artificial life support had neither. Grass to her knees, which meant that she had to walk with care, lest she step on a critter, locate a predator, or fall into a den hole of some sort.

Cameron focused on her mission and let the scientists handle their side of things.

15

Nicodemus Whitlaw wanted to pinch himself as he stepped down the ramp and actually stood on alien soil.

To have come so far. Done so much. Endured the trials and punishments that had seen him stripped of tenure, sentenced to labor camps, and eventually exiled.

And he was here.

He turned to Stevedore Lynch, but words were simply inadequate to express the emotions roiling in his chest. Her smile and nod, however, conveyed some understanding.

Even Renshaw's passive-aggressive bitching on the flight down hadn't put a damper on things, but Gary simply wanted to spend all his time in space, looking for his surfers. Nicodemus couldn't fault him. They shared an ideological inflexibility, after all.

Nicodemus had been the one struck by lightning. Nothing more than that.

He staggered to a halt at the bottom of the ramp, then got tugged off to one side by Lynch as sailors started carrying boxes and bags down out of the shuttle. She led him towards a small hump. Not even a meter above the soil around them, but enough for him to see the true destination of all this in the distance.

So close!

And yet, still tantalizingly beyond his reach. At least for the immediate present.

Armiger Nevin seemed to be in charge for now, issuing orders and answering questions, though Nicodemus had been given to understand that Lynch would command the base.

How? How had the wyrm turned such that he was here?

Nicodemus didn't know. Couldn't.

He could make the most of it.

Quickly, a camp got laid out around him. One tent for cooking. Other tents for sleeping, both with soft sides that could be made rigid by applying a small electrical current when they were deployed, adding a layer of stability and protection. He could see the whole taking shape and it astounded him.

Eventually, he found his voice, uncertain as to where he had lost it.

"How soon?" he asked Kaitlin Lynch.

She nodded and smiled up at him.

"Not long," she replied. "I thought you might like a few moments to recover."

In that, she perhaps knew him better than anyone else, but hadn't she explained that her job involved understanding strangers flying with *Marrakesh* and getting them to know how a starship operated?

"Thank you," he said. "Now, I am like a child on their birthday, seeing presents and a cake and bouncing with excitement."

"I know," she smiled, then turned to one of the nearby groups. "Nevin!"

The Gunnery Officer stopped his conversation and turned. "Sir?"

"The Professor would like to take a preliminary tour of the proposed dig site, Armiger," Lynch called. "Could you organize a team and handle it?"

"Immediately," he nodded. "Farrell."

The tall woman sailor in charge of physical security

approached at a jog. An amazingly tall and strong woman. Intimidating, too, because she knew it and used it as a tool.

Nicodemus preferred women smaller and somewhat mousy. Less crazy versions of Benton, perhaps, though she'd been a willing partner a few times on the flight out.

"Field duty, Farrell," Nevin said simply. "Escorting a group to the dig, walking around, coming back. I'll be with you. So will the Professor."

"Hoàng, you've got base camp," Farrell said to a small woman with Asian features.

Nicodemus found himself in the middle of a whirlwind as Nevin, Farrell, and several sailors grouped up around him, some adding small backpacks.

He looked around at the people he had brought.

"Gary, a walk will do you good," he called to Renshaw, watching the man roll his eyes.

They had an old relationship. Never at odds, because they wanted different things, but never that close, either. Even the flight to Sabahattin hadn't really made them more than fellow travelers.

Still, Renshaw had a first-rate mind when he wanted to actually think. Valuable, in this situation.

"You ready, Professor?" Nevin asked.

Nicodemus studied the brown-haired officer. Darker skin than someone from *Wronlori* generally had. And Nicodemus noted that while Nevin was shorter, he might weigh more than Nicodemus, the result of muscles and a breadth of shoulders that hadn't really been noticeable before.

There was a hint of danger in the air today, though. Personal security and safety was a much higher concern.

"I am," Nicodemus replied. "How do we proceed?"

"Farrell, you're on point?" Nevin turned to the tall woman.

"That's Murphy," she replied. "He's a better cook than gunman, but he makes a good scout."

"Murphy, walking pace," Nevin called out.

Nicodemus fell in beside the man, with Farrell on his other side, though not all that close. The one apparently called Murphy led. Everyone was armed except him and Gary, but that was fine.

What kind of trouble could an academic get into on a world like this?

16

Maddox had added a rainshell over his normal uniform. And a holster, but he wasn't planning to shoot anything today, unless things got really bad. And he had no doubts that Trinh Hoàng would be atop stretched out atop one of the shuttles with her Light Disruptor Cannon on its bipod, watching through a scope at the first hint of a problem. It had the range from here.

He was exercising independent command, as Captain Boru had intended. And learning how to do survey work on the surface of a planet, because they did that a lot, too.

Current terrain: meadow. Sort of. Slowly undulating grasslands nearly thigh-high in places, with the land sloping a little to his left beyond a few small stands of trees, then a steeper drop to the river valley below. Temperature a crisp seventeen degrees, with high clouds but no rain in the immediate forecast. Visibility several kilometers in all directions.

Specialist Murphy on point, leading the group of a dozen folks, a ring of armed sailors as security, a few folks along for technical analysis, and him walking next to Professor Whitlaw, plus Renshaw and a civilian named Tyemir Koviranov who claimed more training with archaeology than the folks who had sat in a class for four hours learning.

Good enough.

Maddox could see how the ground ahead of him started a little uphill, then seemed to turn perfectly flat. It was like a deck almost, though covered over with turf.

The manual he'd been studying recently suggested that it had to have been scraped clean at some previous time to have that sort of perfect level. Then enough time had passed for blowing dirt to accumulate. No trees. The lumps that Radio thought were ships, likely buried the same as the land.

He turned to the Professor as they walked, catching the older man's eye.

"Are we likely to find some sort of bitumen macadam roadway, if we dig down right now and clear away some surface layers of soil?" Maddox asked.

The Professor's step staggered, then caught up again.

Then he blinked in surprise before he answered, probably unprepared for a ship's Gunnery Officer to even know those words, let alone use them properly in conversation.

"That is actually highly likely, Armiger Nevin," he replied. "I was thinking of the ship or ships, but they must exist in a context, and most such contexts would involve some sort of starport, I suppose."

"Agreed, sir," Maddox said. "I was looking at how flat everything is here. That has to be artificial, which led me to expect that maybe we're about to enter what used to be a landing field of some sort. Do we know anything about the people who might have built it?"

"We do not," Whitlaw shook his head as they walked. "The datacore suggests that the ship was seen four hundred standard years ago, but active starflight in this sector of the galaxy goes back at least two thousand years. Maybe more, but we've lost those records as well."

Maddox considered that. Nobody knew where people originally came from. And history of anything prior to *Naara* simply discussed a thing they called *The Scattering*, at least in the books Radio had brought along for everyone to read for background.

The Scattering suggested something even older that people were escaping *from*. Something or someplace people had left behind, eventually landing on places like Igen, the current capital world of the *Holy Imperium of Copez*.

Where? *When?* might be an even better question to ask, but supposedly a competent archaeological dig could answer those questions close enough for Maddox's curiosity.

He caught Farrell's eye.

"At some point, I'll want a patrol to check if they can locate the edges of the potential landing field," he said. "Maybe we'll walk it. And I'll take one of the shuttles up high enough to see if anything stands out. Remind me to ping Squire Taggart and ask what she can determine from orbit."

"Aye, sir," she replied. "I'll add that to my rounds, once we start digging here."

Maddox nodded. That was right out of the book, as well. Send folks out to establish the actual edges of whatever you might be looking at, instead of focusing entirely on the shiny thing at the center. If this had been a starport, there should be buildings. Or at least the remains of them. Maybe hangars for smaller ships. Machine shops and control spaces that might have survived enough to be identified, even if nothing worked today.

Exoarchaeology was a slow, careful thing, but they weren't here to engage in a full and professional dig. This was to prove that the Professor was right, and to convince the Fleet and maybe a few universities to send bigger groups next time. Maybe establish some sort of forward base here to figure out who had once lived on this planet, and what had happened to them.

Maddox couldn't wait.

17

—————

Cameron noted the large lumps in the dirt as they approached. Those things stood out all the more once the Armiger pointed out how flat everything else was, so she presumed buried ships. Or buildings.

Something important enough to uncover. And justify the expedition.

Not today's mission.

Right now, she had to determine if any dangerous critters had chosen to live in the immediate vicinity and needed to be dealt with. Things that didn't know to be afraid of humans and immediately take off running the other direction when she showed up.

The Adjustable Disruptor was set to maximum range, because she felt like teaching things whatever manners they needed from a significant distance. So far, nothing. Not even really game trails, but if this was pavement with grass growing over it, she could see where things might only bed down, then move on.

At least until they got close to the lumps. Then it would get tricky.

Cameron estimated the closest lump to be roughly one hundred and seventy-five meters long. Maybe fifteen meters tall, so if it was a ship, she was looking at either three or four decks, depending whether the landing gear had collapsed at some point.

Hafta dig it out to know.

Still, the dimensions suggested something about the size of a corvette, if it was one ship under there. Two, if it was cutters of some sort, lined up nose to tail.

Cameron turned to Armiger Nevin.

"Sir, do we know how many lumps we're looking at?" she asked.

"Scan says eight of them, Farrell," he replied. "Metal underneath, but we could be detecting either the hull of a ship or just buildings. We'll get there, then take a walk clockwise to see what sort of perimeter we need to hold. Don't know yet if we'll move *Crime Lab* over here to provide a forward base. You and Lynch will make that call."

She liked that he left it at that. The Stevedore was in charge of the operations on the surface. She handled security. He was an officer, but not being a pain in the ass about that and letting her determine things herself based on her expertise.

No trees anywhere close, which made sense if this was a base. They might have put down an impermeable barrier at some ancient point. Might have treated the ground to prevent roots. Something, because even the grass was suddenly shorter, barely coming up to his ankle.

Huh.

"Sir," she called. "We just crossed a boundary line."

Cameron pointed. She could even see it, stopped and turning sideways. Pretty damned straight, looking longways down it, but from above you might have to see shadows in the afternoon to notice.

Still, more proof that it was artificial.

"Good catch, Farrell," Nevin replied. "Everyone look sharp and pay attention for any artifacts that might be only partially buried."

"We expecting anything?" Murphy called from up front.

"Negative, but if they left crap around, that makes it easier," he replied.

She watched the man turn to the Professor.

"Did you think to bring a metal detector with you?" he asked.

She could see where she'd confused the man.

"No?" the Professor replied. "Why?"

"Dirt over anything useful," Nevin stated. "But possibly pretty shallow, depending. Useful to be able to locate it. Especially buried wires that might lead us to more interesting things."

Huh. Cameron hadn't thought about that.

At the same time, her job was shooting things that needed shooting. Not digging. She was handling base and operational security for Lynch, with her team largely not involved at all on the functional side of things. Instead, they'd be back to quartermaster and cooking duties, just on the ground instead of the ship.

They walked.

Yup, eight lumps. Couple much wider, suggesting buildings that had maybe collapsed at some point. Low and lumpy.

"Murphy, hold here," she called, catching out of the corner of her eye one thing she wanted to see closer.

"What have you got, Farrell?" Armiger Nevin asked.

She pointed.

"Walking up on top of that to see what vantage the height gives me, sir," she replied.

"Good idea," he said. "I'll come with you."

Cameron nodded and led. The grass had marks like water flowing out of a small bowl, but no pond. Just a lump of green dough about five meters tall on one corner, then below that elsewhere.

She could see a considerable distance in two directions, with the other lumps more or less blocking her sight on the other two. Still, a good place to put a watcher, to see what there while looking farther east. Mostly more grass rolling away, but somewhere over there it started to tumble down to the valley and the sea shore.

"This feel square to you, sir?" she asked, looking down.

He knelt and looked right and left.

"Yes, but I'm not sure how easy it will be to see what there is underneath," he said.

"Maybe a crane with a bucket?" she asked, mostly as a lark, but his eyes got way serious for a moment.

"Yes," he replied, standing. "Excellent idea, Farrell. I'll ask Jareth Ahearn to build us something and send it down with a future cargo run."

Cameron shrugged. It sounded like his idea, but she wouldn't ever turn down a gold star next to her name on a report to the Captain. Or anyone else.

"Let's finish our pass," she offered, moving back to lower ground.

Because a tower over all this might give her a great place to keep watch from. Put it on wheels or treads and roll it over to wherever you wanted to dig, and you could kill a whole lot of birds with one stone.

And have an adventure along the way.

18

———

Padraig signed off and considered Kaitlin's words as he looked around his bridge.

Camp established. Perimeter in the process of being built up around their landing area, with plans to do something similar over there at the dig itself once they had a better idea about what they were looking at.

And already the first list of things they'd forgotten about or never once considered before now.

Maddox sounded like he was making a mental transition, which was a shame, but also the nature of things. Especially when the rest of the Fleet was at war. Padraig would miss him, but the Fleet would be in a better place by putting that man in command somewhere.

He keyed in a number.

"Messier," Chance said from her cabin.

She'd only gone off duty a few minutes ago, and Padraig knew she wouldn't sleep for several more hours.

"It's Padraig," he replied. "Where have you gotten with your thoughts on doing a deeper survey of the Sabahattin system? Our folks are down and settling in at present."

"I'm of two minds, Padraig," she said. "It would probably be best to keep scanning the ground to see what the rest of the planet tells us. I'd say we drop a probe right here to act as a communications relay so we can move around. Was there anything else interesting we flew by?"

"Taggart is scanning everything and using passive optical, but nothing has stood out yet," he told her. "If there were artificial satellites in orbit at some point, they've fallen or been swept away."

"Have we looked in the LaGrange points?" Chance asked.

"She has, but not gotten any active signals," he acknowledged. "Lots of things that might look interesting if we sailed over and got a better view. I agree with you that we should schedule that as third priority, after orbit and ground. The rest of the planetary system can wait until after that."

"What do you need me to concentrate on?" Chance pressed.

"Kaitlin and Maddox sent up a list of stuff they want on the ground," Padraig said. "Some of it we'll need to fabricate from bar and sheet stock. Some will be electronic gear that Taggart's people can do. I'd like to turn over that portion to you to supervise, Chance, so I can concentrate on doing a full survey of everything around here."

"I'm on it," she said. "Jareth got the list?"

"He's asleep, so I gave it to Rod Garber," Padraig laughed. "I got the feeling that they are in a race to see how much of it they can have done before the Engineer actually comes back on duty."

Chance laughed as well.

"Yeah, I can see that with those folks," she said. "I'll head aft and check in. Anything else?"

"No, we're playing this one a little loose because we are in the middle of nowhere," he said. "Log everything so folks can complain later about whatever they think we should have been doing, but we've got a blank slate to work with here."

"Got it," she replied. "I'll leave you notes before I go to bed."

"We'll talk more tomorrow," he said, and cut the line.

Right now, he was pulling a long shift because he had

Maddox on the ground training on how to be a survey officer while Nyssa spent every available minute off-duty crunching data.

In fact...

He dialed another number.

"Astro-telemetry," Nyssa replied. "Taggart."

"It's Captain Boru," he said. "I'd like to make you get up from the chair, walk all the way to the Bridge for some exercise, and brief me."

Knowing her, she'd been in that chair for hours, hunched over and clicking through the logs, or writing code to filter things based on whatever interpretation might sound interesting.

There was a reason he let her run wild with that sort of data. She could find things nobody else could.

"Be right there, sir," she replied.

Padraig keyed another number.

"Wardroom."

"It's the Captain," he said. "I'd like a carafe of coffee and two mugs delivered to my day office, please."

"Right away, sir."

He sat back and watched. Main screen showed the curve of Sabahattin's horizon, static as *Marrakesh* was remaining in place overhead as the world turned. Nothing on the Aetherial Scanners as far as they could spot, but he hadn't expected anything.

He dialed a number.

"Secondary Bridge. Magorian."

"Bex, it's Captain Boru. I'm going into a meeting in my office shortly. You assume temporary watch and call me if anything out of the ordinary occurs. Or Commander Messier, who should be in Engineering."

"Understood, sir."

The steward pushing a cart and Nyssa arrived together, so he rose and nodded.

"In my office."

19

———

Nyssa hadn't realized how stiff she was until she'd stood up. Or how tired until she smelled that coffee and some little light came on in the back of her head.

But he was the Captain for a reason. And did everything he could to make sure people were ready, fit, and fully trained to react to any circumstances.

Like studying all night for a test. That was what this felt like.

But he didn't speak. Merely sipped at his mug while she did the same, discovering that she was also a little chilled so that hot coffee hit bottom and spread out like a warm blanket.

"Better?" he finally asked.

"Yes, sir," she admitted. "Might have squirreled in a little hard."

He chuckled.

"Gosh, Radio, that's so out of character for you."

Nyssa blushed. He knew her better than her parents did, but that wasn't a particularly high bar, come to think of it.

She grinned wryly and shrugged.

"Anything interesting come up?" Captain Boru asked.

"Not so far, sir," she replied, framing things in her head. "I found several spots that might qualify as crossroads, assuming one was shipping cargo between *Traisa* and *Wronlori*, but we didn't stay anywhere long enough to pick up any ships in flight."

"What about piracy?" he asked.

"Sir?"

"If you can find those spots, bad guys can find them, too, Nyssa," he nodded. "Or privateers, if Fleet put a commerce raider ship out here somewhere to disrupt *Wronlori* trade. Where would you put a base, if you wanted to make it quiet and out of the way?"

Nyssa blinked and took a deep drink. She'd been thinking about this in terms of survey stuff, because Maddox had asked her a whole list of new questions she'd never heard come out of his mouth before. And Gunnery Officer Nevin had changed into someone else to ask them, because warfighting hadn't actually come up.

She wasn't sure she recognized this new Maddox.

"I can think of a few places, sir," she offered, reviewing data in her head. "Would they operate out this far?"

"Turn it on its head, Squire," he countered. "We know about *A'Zedi*, *Wronlori*, and *Traisa* in this direction. But as Professor Whitlaw points out, organized starflight in this region dates back at least two thousand years, as well as several civilizations."

"In this region, sir?" she asked.

"*Naara* was founded after *The Scattering*, Radio," he answered. "Who scattered? Where did they come from before that? Presumably, the regions beyond *Copez* going upstream and possibly coreward, which is almost exactly the opposite of where we are today. At the same time, a scattering suggests a dandelion throwing seeds in the air. Where else might folks have landed?"

"And Sabahattin?"

"What's beyond us here?" Captain Boru asked. "Who might we encounter if we kept sailing outward on this vector?"

"Nobody immediately close, sir," she replied. "Lots of zones where the stars get thinner. Not empty, but one main sequence star every fifteen or twenty light-years, instead of clustered together like we're used to. I suppose someone might choose to settle on some dim red star, if they wanted to remain hidden, but I can't imagine they'd want to live there long term. As for piracy? Some base in the middle of nowhere? I can look."

"Do that," he nodded. "We've got the probes watching *Wron-lori*, so I'm not worried about someone sneaking up on us from over there. And we'll need to put one down right here so the ship can move and start a closer scan of the rest of the surface, in case we've missed anything so far. Remember, this world was inhabited long enough to have some sort of base built on the surface at some point. Obviously, they left later, but what did they leave behind?"

"I don't know, sir," Nyssa admitted.

"Nor do I expect you to, Nyssa," he replied. "We've got time, and you're on point to find things for us, because I'm pretty sure that this mission is already wildly successful for merely having located whatever it is on the ground. What else can we find? Mostly, however, I figured that you needed a break, so I dragged you in here for some coffee."

She watched him rise, gesturing her to remain seated as he grabbed his own mug.

"You take a few minutes and enjoy your break, Squire," he ordered with a smile. "Then get back to duty, but remember that you don't have to do it all today."

Then he left her alone in the office. Nyssa refilled her mug and considered everything he had just told her. And recentered that map she kept in her head.

Up until now, she'd marked Sabahattin on the bottom right edge. The Rimward and Spinward corner. But that was wrong, as Captain Boru had pointed out, so she drew back some and expanded that corner to show all sorts of other space where there might be interesting things to see.

And nobody they knew had ever even come this far.

What might be out there beyond?

Food for thought.

In fact, her stomach rumbling reminded her that she hadn't eaten in hours either, too focused on the trees that were her data and not seeing the forest of information hidden there.

She rose and nodded to the Captain's ghost.

Time to fix that.

20

———

Maddox had slept well. And still gotten up early, rising with ship-time that wasn't quite aligned with the planet. At least not yet. If *Marrakesh* stayed in orbit overhead long enough, he knew that Captain Boru would adjust everything, rather than making people on the ground stay on his schedule.

That was what a good commanding officer did.

The sun was just rising as he emerged from the tent, quiet because a lot of other folks had been too excited to go to sleep early last night.

The wardroom crew had their own tent on the other side of the mess hall tent, where they had no doubt gotten up in the middle of the night to start prepping for feeding hungry diggers.

Lots of stars overhead, so the front had passed. Cool verging on crisp this morning. Maddox slipped hands into his jacket pockets and made sure he'd packed gloves and a pullover cap in case he needed them.

A quick bio-break and he was in line for food behind the Professor and the skinny guy. Renshaw. Space Surfers.

Weird, but no weirder than lost starships landed or crashed on an abandoned planet, so Maddox was willing to give the man the benefit of the doubt. Just because current interstellar science had no way to explain it didn't mean that it was impossible.

Hell, starflight had once been considered impossible.

Oatmeal with spices and dried fruit this morning. Easy, bulky protein and a way to get all sorts of trace vitamins and minerals into folks expecting to burn a lot of calories today. Coffee because caffeine for an early morning.

He followed the two civilians to a trestle table and joined them.

"Armiger?" Renshaw asked. "What gets you up so early?"

"Planning to dig today," Maddox replied, watching both men apparently frown at the thought of an officer getting his hands dirty.

But you gotta get in the thick of things to learn. And Maddox wanted to learn.

"Interesting," Professor Whitlaw managed. "Is this normal?"

"Captain Boru sets high standards for his crew, sir," Maddox replied, feeling the honest truth of those words as he spoke them. "Examples that show the rest of us how it should be done. Plus, I want to be able to touch that hull when we get down to metal and find it. Were you planning to dig into that biggest lump first?"

"I was," Whitlaw nodded, starting to eat and talk at the same time. "We'll start in roughly ten meters from the north end and go down from the top. That lets us work to that end of what is likely the hull once we see what's under there."

"Do you have a way to identify a ship, just from uncovering a square meter of hull?" Renshaw asked before Maddox could.

Whitlaw smiled.

"One of my best kept secrets," he admitted. "I have been accumulating records of every known class of starship built and storing them in my datacore. There are gaps, obviously. Especially for modern ships that have security clearances around them, but I've always been more interested in the ancients anyway, so we ought to be able to get a good start. And once we clear the aft and get to whatever thrusters they used, I'll be in even better shape."

Maddox nodded. Renshaw seemed unconvinced.

"Question for you, Mr. Renshaw," Maddox intruded. "How would you expect surfboards would work in space?"

He sat back and shoveled food into his mouth as the small man got a gleam in his eyes.

"On a planetary, oceanic surface, they work by harnessing energy differentials from a wave being driven into the shallows and curling over to crash on the sand," Renshaw replied. "Extrapolating outwards, there are suggestions that the gravity that binds all things together might also be able to be utilized. Differentials between large and small objects thus create attractive forces that could be tapped. Like a ship on the surface of an ocean with sails, we thus expect that surfers could tack or run on those gravity swells."

"Interesting," Maddox offered, realizing that the man was both smart and educated, just not entirely normal. If anybody really was, when you got down to it. "And how would you cross interstellar distances? We use the Ghostdrive to achieve a medium FTL. Without that, you are functionally trapped in a single system. Or sailing for centuries at a time, at which point would we be dealing with immortal beings? Possibly folks indistinguishable from gods?"

"There are two schools of thought there, Armiger Nevin," Renshaw replied sagely. "One holds to sublight travel and measures prospective lifespans in millennia. I feel that such beings ought to be able to tap into something like Ghost-space, if not the same place, and perhaps ride whatever dimensional differential energy exists. Our own ships have to generate a field that drives the vessel up and out of our space, holding it at those same FTL speeds, so the theory would work the same. If we presume the surfers are wearing some sort of suit, perhaps permanently bonded to their skin like an armor, then they would have the ability to travel in a manner close enough to our understanding. Does that help?"

Maddox chewed and considered. On the surface of things,

completely insane, but once you started tugging on threads, all of it was at least grounded in what felt like an internally consistent logic.

Nuts, but stable.

"It does, sir," he replied. "How would you build sensors to locate the surfers or their boards?"

"I beg your pardon?" Renshaw asked, suddenly leaning forward in confusion.

"We have our Aetherial Scanners to locate other ships in Ghost-space," Maddox replied with a nod. "The waves ping up into that space and are thus fast FTL, frequently ranging at a speed of roughly fifty light-years per hour, though of a relatively short overall distance. To locate them, either they would appear on our sensors, in which case I would have expected to find them and potentially communicate already, or they are using a different phase of Ghost-space, which might be better—possibly faster—for us to use as well."

He left it at thar. Captain Boru reminded all of his officers and crew to keep open minds about things, rather than simply disregarding them. Especially with some of the weirder ideas that had percolated with the current mission.

But if you turned it into a scientific study, what could you find? Even if you didn't locate those surfers, could you create better scanners looking for them? Faster FTL drives because you spent so much time trying to do it a different way than everybody did today?

What were the limits of dreaming?

Renshaw was at a loss. Whitlaw stepped in and rescued him.

"Better scanners, Armiger Nevin?" the Professor asked.

"Aye, sir," Maddox nodded. "If you don't locate them today, you might still move the current state of technology forward. In fact, that's the sort of thing that I suspect the Fleet might get behind with funding, if you framed it in those terms. Much as you got a grant because an old starship might be technologically interesting, in which case the Fleet would want to know, because better tech should be a thing they want. I don't know, but obviously when you get back, Mr. Renshaw, there ought to be opportunities to talk to folks."

Both men sat there gobsmacked.

Maddox got it. Most of the crew looked at this whole expedition as a lark. Fleet funding wackos and crackpots. However, that didn't mean that Gary Renshaw might not come up with an idea that revolutionized...well, everything.

He kept shoveling food, getting ready to go out with the first group, as soon as things were ready.

Maddox also wanted to see that future.

This morning, it might start in the distant past.

21

———

Nicodemus followed the sailors from *Marrakesh* who were keeping him protected from whatever might live on Sabahattin. And felt safer for it.

He doubted that there would be many problems with claim jumpers, and could always make it a point to inspect all of his assistants for stolen goods on the way home if he had the need. At the same time, there wasn't much that they could carry off without someone noticing, unless the sailors got involved and somehow convinced the Captain and his officers to do it.

They might have those sorts of orders, but he'd be willing to risk that, after talking so much with Kaitlin and Armiger Nevin. Hell, even Gary Renshaw had taken him aside after breakfast, slightly giddy with some of Nevin's ideas and how they might be implemented.

Nicodemus lacked the electronics background to be of much help, but perhaps Darlene Wellington could assist. She had the training, from what Nicodemus remembered.

He was still a little surprised at how seriously everyone was taking these ideas. *Wronlori* had laughed him out of a job, out of a life, and even out of his home, because he dreamed of the past.

A'Zedi had accepted him, coddled him, and was now financing him.

The lump grew larger as they walked, already the grass path starting to get matted down and eventually pounded into a trail connecting the small landing base with the digging space. And he needed the gap between the two bases, because landing thrusters on shuttles tended to kick up a lot of dust and grit. He'd hate to recover something fragile, then have a wave of thruster overpressure or wind crack it after being however long hidden from mankind.

They crossed onto the space Nevin had considered the edge of a landing field from the way the grass seemed to grow shorter. Nicodemus was tempted to start a dig here, just to answer that question, but he had a dragon buried over there and wanted that siren song answered so much more.

Nevin stopped him anyway.

"Should we excavate here?" the sailor asked.

"I'm starting the preliminary dig there," Nicodemus pointed.

"Understood, sir," Nevin nodded. "I can detach a couple of my folks here, with instructions to exercise care and stop when they hit whatever is there."

Nicodemus considered it.

So much to do, and so little time, because *Marrakesh* had an exact number of days before they had to depart for resupply at an *A'Zedi* base or call for another ship to carry more food to them here. Weeks, but only weeks. He'd even considered planting food crops, but that would require pulling his people off the dig. And he had no idea what would grow here. Or how quickly.

"Go ahead, Armiger," Nicodemus decided. "I'd like to know myself."

Nevin smiled and indicated a nearby sailor, pointing the man to a spot nearby and indicating the shape and direction of the hole he wanted dug.

Nicodemus chivied the rest into motion, that last hundred meters to the ancient burial ground he had dreamed about last night. They got close, and he began organizing the on-site dig controls. Where *Crime Lab* would land. Where folks would put up tents to rest during the day and perhaps overnight rather than walking back and forth. Where latrines would be dug. All the little things.

The creek wasn't close, but that was good, as it would protect the artifacts underground. And folks were drinking water that had been treated aboard *Marrakesh* because nobody knew what germs and bugs might live on this planet.

There were limits to how much you could boost your immune system, and he expected everyone on the ground to have some manner of sniffles and colds, just adapting. They would all be treated before being allowed back to orbit to protect that crew.

Just in case.

The hours flew by quickly, while also grinding, but after a quick lunch, they had everything organized on the ground below and Nicodemus had led the first team of diggers to the top of the hill. To that spot that should be close to the overhead engineering hatch on any landable starship.

The view from up here was a dream come true. Nicodemus marked the spot after pacing several times and reviewing his Monitoring Datalog, the handheld device he had homebrewed back home when he had had a research budget for digs. It handled all of the sensing, recording, and computing he needed, with a variety of tools built in.

Mostly, though, he was all about the low-tech process. Picks and shovels working down to hand trowels and dust brushes. Tarps that he could spread out every night to keep moisture and rain off the dig. Rulers and cameras to record everything *in situ* before it got transferred to *Crime Lab* and cleaned up.

He'd even brought a small hot air balloon they could inflate, in order to provide a look-down capability for a camera, without having to hover a shuttle where it might damage anything or use an expensive remote-controlled drone.

And paper to sketch it all.

So primitive for interstellar exoarchaeology. But exactly how you went about doing it.

"Remember," he told Nevin and Yves Harcrow, the two who would be doing the initial digging, "slowly for now, sorting each shovel into the bucket, where the second team will sift it for anything interesting, as well as removing it from the dig entirely and placing it off to the side out of the way."

"Indeed, Professor," Yves nodded, starting in with a shovel that hadn't advanced much technologically from the beginning of any Iron Age.

Nicodemus moved closer towards the probable bow to watch and wait. Kaitlin Lynch had thought to bring a pair of folding campaign chairs, cloth stretched on frames, and an umbrella to keep the afternoon sun off of them, though she'd left it collapsed because the air was just barely above a chill.

Good for the diggers and people moving around. He'd need something hot occasionally to drink.

They sat, watching and waiting in companionable silence as the stronger men dug.

22

———

Kaitlin had left Athyn Kera in charge, back at the camp, with about half of Cameron's security folks. While only a specialist and a cook, Kera was still a good person to keep that chunk of operations in motion while Kaitlin played a bit of hooky and watched the dig from up close.

Later, she would split her time between the two sites, getting in a lot of walking that she probably needed, but right now history was going to be made, however small or large it turned out to be.

They'd been at it all afternoon, Maddox and Yves splitting off and swapping with a few others until there was a hole about half a meter deep by two meters wide. The sudden hollow ***thunk*** stopped everybody, bodies unexpectedly jumping, in spite of knowing that they were close.

Maddox had been in the hole. He looked up at Nicodemus as the Professor practically exploded into motion in spite of how relaxed he had probably appeared to everyone else.

Kaitlin had been close enough to watch his hands fidget.

Yves backed up and Maddox moved to one side below as Nicodemus plunged into the hole like a wolf pouncing on a wounded rabbit. Everyone else was either moving closer or looking up from the ground below.

Kaitlin moved slower, standing and walking, noting how low the sun was on the horizon. Not sunset, but everyone still had a cleanup period here, then the walk back to camp, dinner, and possibly showers if those had gotten properly deployed.

Clean water and heat were the issue. You could bathe in the creek if you wanted, but it was only a few degrees above freezing. Better to pump it into a tank, treat it, then heat it.

Kaitlin figured she could live for a few days with a funk, considering how dirty everyone else was going to be.

Nicodemus disappeared from sight, so she walked closer.

"Bucket!" he yelled, and Yves lowered an empty one into the hole.

She watched the Professor scrape by hand, placing individual clumps of dirt into the bucket like a badger digging a den. She smiled at the image.

Thunk, thunk, thunk.

Contact with whatever was under the hole. Metal. Hollow enough to echo, suggesting a space beneath that was intact. Soil could be heavy when it got wet, but starships were designed for much greater loads, so if it had just been landed and forgotten, it could be intact.

Hopefully.

Everyone waited with bated breath as Nicodemus worked. Then his head popped up.

"Gary, join me!" he yelled, surprising Renshaw even more than everyone else, but the tiny man quickly made his way up the slope to the lip of the hole.

"Yes, you," Nicodemus said when Gary stood surprised on the edge of the hole. "Come, see it. Feel it. Know some joy in your life and imagine what these Navy people might be able to do for you!"

Kaitlin caught Maddox's glance and nodded. She'd heard about the conversation over breakfast and approved wholeheartedly at what the young man had said to the civilians.

Give the rest of them the potential to dream, if they could find a way to filter it through what the Fleet might fund for research.

Weirder things had happened.

Both men swished dirt away from a gray, metallic hull. Lighter in hue than what *A'Zedi* would manufacture, but that might be the alloy itself, being buried for so long that molecules in the soil could have bonded bond to the metal and changed the color.

Time passed as the two men worked. Kaitlin's comm beeped loudly, another jolt of mad energy causing the entire crowd to jump.

"Kaitlin," she said, answering.

"Dinner bell is going off," Athyn replied. "If you want it warm, you might want to start walking this way. Or you can have cold leftovers, but I'm eating without you."

Kaitlin laughed.

"Shortly," she promised, wondering if she was lying, then looked down at the men in the hole.

"Tarps!" Nicodemus hollered, causing people to suddenly race up with the things in hand and start unfolding them.

Protect the dig from rain and mist, though it had been clear today. Also from any moisture accumulating below and damaging anything that might have survived this long. Nicodemus and Gary were out of the hole on opposite sides, keeping a sharp, professional running commentary as they directed the others into placing it just so and then weighing it down with dirt that had been bucketed for just this occasion.

The hole was obvious but covered. Nicodemus nodded, then turned in place.

"Thank you, all of you," he called to the group, civilian and Navy alike. "We have come this far and seen the thing. Tomorrow, we will start exposing it and hopefully get far enough to identify what it is. I intend to be up early, breaking my fast so I can dig at first light. *Crime Lab* will be locked for now, and busy tomorrow, so start pacing yourselves because we will work sun to sun starting tomorrow, with a crew putting in the fence we hope will keep out wildlife. Now, let us return and have dinner to celebrate, my friends. We have already accomplished the impossible, and it only gets better from here."

Kaitlin wasn't sure she agreed with the words, but the sentiment was good. And would drive folks to greater heights.

And maybe, just maybe, there was a starship under there that they could excavate.

How amazing would that be?

23

———

Cameron had been asleep, but someone touching the bottom of her foot softly had her up, out of the bag, and pointing a weapon before she had actually opened her eyes and processed what was going on.

Murphy, squatting at the foot of her cot, nodding as Cameron shook her head once to clear it.

Dark outside, but those two moons weren't for shit when it came to lighting things. She'd had a mast raised in the middle of the camp with a light on the top to at least let people see if they had to hit the latrines in the darkness.

"Status?" she whispered, hoping she could let the others in here sleep.

Big tent. Some folks snored. Others squeaked. Murphy nodded and rose, gesturing her to follow.

Cameron dropped her feet into her boots, holstered the Adjustable Disruptor, and stood, grabbing her jacket from under the cot where she'd stashed it.

Outside. Cold air. Cold, white light, omnidirectional. Bit of fog in some of the low places. Smaller moon overhead, winking.

She noted that Murphy was looking a little furtive.

"Movement outside the wire, Top," he whispered, leaning

close and turned such a way that they were watching the dig in the distance, though it was just a darker spot.

"Fence intact?" she asked, glancing around.

The other team had spent the day driving posts with a small hydraulic crane on the back of a rolling cart. Something the Engineer had dreamed up on the way here, adapting a cargo lifter. Really easy way to enclose the hectare that was the main camp, with the shuttles landing outside that and locked up tight.

Cyclone fencing was open enough you could see right through it. And shoot, too, if you had to. Climbable by most things that could handle trees, but noisy in the process, and Cameron had teams specifically on the ground to walk patrols, plus motion sensors everywhere, keeping eyes outbound.

"Nobody has approached the compound, Top," Murphy said quietly. "Sensors picked up something closer to the dig. We didn't have anything that could range that far, so all we got were some fuzzy warm spots moving around. Maybe people sized. Or bears. This planet inhabited?"

"Nobody knows, Murph," she nodded. "Bridge didn't find any radio communications or city lights from orbit, but that's civilization-level shit. There might be primitives moving around. And there might be bears or wolves that smelled all the people moving around and wondered if we were tasty."

"They're in for a bit of a shock if they come this way," Murphy laughed dryly. "Too many ghost stories have got folks maybe a little too ready to shoot first, then wait for light to ask questions."

"Safer that way," she agreed, knowing that Nevin and Captain Boru might disagree, but they'd put her in charge down here, so security would be done the right way. "If the sensors pick up anything getting close, sound the alert, but don't shoot until they make a hostile move. Might be a weird-ass first contact. Might be sharks sniffing. Fence won't keep them out for long, but the whole idea is to draw a line in the sand that we'll hold."

"Figured you needed to know," Murphy nodded. "No immediate threats here, and folks have stepped their watchfulness up a level."

"Let the cooking crew know when they wake up," she ordered. "Then be prepared in case we've got an expedition. Maybe taking the shuttle up and seeing if its scanners can do anything."

"*Marrakesh* help?"

"Doubt it," she shook her head. "They'd need light, same as us, unless they dropped way low in orbit and hovered. We'll see what our visitors did when we have light. I'll update the officers. You keep the patrols running."

"You going to try sleeping?" he asked.

Cameron checked her comm. Middle of the night. Three hours until she would have woken up to be ready with the others.

And the Professor had wanted to be on-site at first light, which meant moving the forward team over there in the darkness.

Ambush time? Folks setting traps to catch the diggers?

Crap and a half.

"No," she decided after a long beat. "Tomorrow's going to be a long day, so let the cooks know to make extra coffee, too. I've got to go wake up the bosses."

24

———

Maddox had slept deeply enough that he was still a little groggy as Farrell drew him out where the bite of the night breeze suddenly ripped all the sleepiness off.

He blinked a few times, realizing how wound up the woman was compared to her normal phlegmatic state.

"What's up?" he finally asked, noting that they had moved clear over to the new fence that had been installed today.

The dig was a dark spot in the distance.

"Sensors picked up movement and heat on the dig site, sir," Farrell said. "When my folks spooked, whatever was over there did as well. Nothing showing right now and not an immediate threat, but we're all supposed to tromp over there in the darkness later so the Professor is ready to dig at first light."

"Any hint as to what it was?" he asked.

"Just warm blobs on the screen," she said, pulling out a tablet and showing him.

At a distance of a kilometer, pixelated warm spots moving, just like she'd said, but this equipment was defensive in nature. Not designed to resolve something at that range, because Farrell had intended them to work as a moat protecting the camp.

Maddox nodded, then pulled out his comm and linked it to the tablet before activating it.

"*Marrakesh*. Magorian."

"Bex, I'm sending you a sensor log that we captured here a little while ago," Maddox said. "See if you can process it and resolve anything with better detail."

"Need to alert Taggart or the Captain, sir?" she asked.

"Exercise your best judgment," Maddox replied. "No apparent threat on the ground at this time. Actually, have the flight deck ready with *Roadrunner*, in case we need it on short notice, either to insert more security personnel or to evac the ground team. And let whoever is in charge know."

"Captain's off duty," Bex replied. "Radio's working late and has the Bridge, but I'm answering all calls at present."

"Route it through her and let her decide," Maddox said. "Might be nothing at my end. Might not be."

"Understood, sir," Magorian said. "Anything else?"

"Negative," Maddox replied. "Out."

He cut the line and nodded to Farrell.

"You stay on top of security," he said. "I'll wake the Professor and the Stevedore and bring them up to speed."

"Understood," Farrell nodded.

Maddox squared his shoulders and headed back to the tent where the officers had been sleeping.

25

Padraig came alert instantly when the comm beeped at him, in spite of a dream involving pancakes. Their smell even lingered when he opened his eyes, so he considered asking the wardroom for a special breakfast later.

Time said an hour after planetary midnight.

"Boru," he said, keying the channel.

"Sir, it's Taggart," Nyssa came over the line. "It is not an emergency, but could you join me on the Bridge?"

There was a fine line to be walked there. Not sounding general quarters and sending the crew racing madly to battle stations, but exploding her commanding officer out of his bed, into his shoes, and out the hatch.

"On my way," he said, already in motion.

Bridge wasn't dark, but it was quiet. Andrea Whelan was on Helm, because the Chief of the Boat could do just about any job there was, lacking perhaps only some of the finer points back in Engineering. Maybe.

Nyssa Taggart was at her station, screens open showing images as he got over her right shoulder to look.

"Nevin called with something on the ground," she began.

"Bex Magorian did a quick analysis, then handed it off to me so I could use some of my more advanced tools on it."

Padraig nodded. In her other role, she'd been trained and equipped to break enemy codes in real time. *Marrakesh* had been quietly seconded to *A'Zedi* Intelligence Services to do spy things, though he'd been expecting this mission to be much more normal.

Whatever normal was.

She also had some *severely* upgraded processing power to throw at a problem like this.

"The images were captured by short-range sensors setting atop the fencing that surrounds the camp," she continued. "Normal useful range is roughly three hundred meters, depending on local conditions and terrain, so they were lucky to see things at just over eleven hundred. The images are fuzzy, but we do know that it was living creatures they detected, because they included thermographic data."

In his mind, they almost looked like stick figures to Padraig, but that was probably just the human response of anthropomorphizing things.

"What am I looking at, Radio?" he asked when she fell silent.

"Sir, they might be people." She turned her dark brown eyes to look directly at him. "We have no evidence of a technological civilization and might have overlooked that the inhabitants could have regressed for some reason."

"Lost the sky?" he asked, hearing the poetry in his words as they came out.

"Possibly, sir," she nodded. "The ship and whatever else was there was buried, so it might have been forgotten. But they might have preserved stories."

"Sounds like a lot of maybe on extremely thin evidence," he countered. Not crushing that element of hope in her voice but framing it professionally.

"Understood, sir," she said. "Maddox also asked us to keep

Roadrunner on ready-to-launch, just in case. Should we prepare to send down some better scanner equipment?"

Padraig paused to consider his options. The Professor had his digging team supplemented by a number of folks from *Marrakesh*, over and above the teams maintaining the camps. He could probably justify adding a few more people down there. That would give Kaitlin and Nevin more options, if they needed to explore or defend the base.

And if there were people down there, however primitive, the status of this planet had just changed radically.

A'Zedi could have placed some claim on the world by showing evidence of the dig. But interstellar mining law presumed uninhabited places. Dead moons or rogue asteroids.

Or uninhabited planets.

Having people might change everything, and he wasn't as prepared as he should be.

Padraig leaned over Nyssa's shoulder and dialed a comm number, letting it ring several times before someone answered.

"Dimitriou," she said, groggy.

But then, the Legal Affairs officer rarely got involved in many things. Usually, she advised on wills and divorces when one of the crew was involved and handled a lot of paperwork.

"It's Captain Boru," he said. "I have a potential situation on my hands and need to consult my expert, but it is not an emergency. Could you join me in my office in half an hour? That gives you time for a shower and some coffee."

"What should I be prepared to discuss, Captain?" she asked, her voice already sharper.

But then, a Legal Affairs officer also sat on Boards of Inquiry, when major punishments might be handed down. That kept the mind sharp.

"Interstellar law dealing with a primitive civilization making a potential First Contact with *A'Zedi*, Squire Dimitriou," Padraig said.

"Oh, shit," she whispered, then caught herself. "I'll be there as quickly as I can, Captain."

"See you then," he said, cutting the line and turning to Cox Whelan.

"Coxswain, I'll need you to hold the fort for a bit," he told her, then turned to Nyssa. "Wake Chance up and have her join us as well. She's probably done everything in all her time on a desk, so she'll have useful ideas."

"Sir, we don't really know anything at this point," Nyssa noted.

"No, but the sun will be up in a few hours, Squire," he replied. "And the folks on the surface might need to know what their options are before then."

She nodded and he moved to his own command station.

"Wardroom."

"This is the Captain," he told them. "I'll need coffee for four and whatever pastries or munchies you can deliver to my office in thirty minutes."

There was a brief pause.

"Understood, sir."

26

Kaitlin had thought that being on the ground would be something of a vacation. A camping trip, as it were. She hadn't been prepared for the fact that she would be in charge if something extraordinary occurred.

Or rather, this extraordinary.

She sipped fresh coffee and listened as Nyssa Taggart finished a quick briefing from orbit. And Kaitlin appreciated that Padraig, Chance, and Squire Dimitriou were also present up on *Marrakesh*, even as early as it was.

Around the table, the Professor and Maddox both fidgeted for different reasons, but Kaitlin was in charge down here, subject only to Padraig overriding her if he felt he had a reason.

And Taggart had just made it clear that Padraig might, but not yet.

It would be in her hands for now.

"Do we know if they are human?" Kaitlin asked the group, both on the screen and around the table, noting that Cam was outside, walking patrol lines with the rest of her people.

"What else would they be?" Nicodemus asked, surprised.

All of them were surprised when she expected Nicodemus to be the most in tune with what others of his group called cryptids.

But she supposed that he was merely a fellow traveler with that group, rather than a true believer like Gary Renshaw or Yuri Nikinov.

"We have a wide spectrum," Kaitlin replied. "A pack of wolves or bears at one end. Animal intelligence, but not tool-making or cultures being passed orally. Descendants of some former travelers at the other end, gone primitive. However, those poles are a great distance apart, so it could be anything in between as well."

"Aliens?" Maddox asked. "Actual non-human intelligent life forms? We've never discovered such, but the Captain has pointed out that we are rather far removed from the various descendant cultures of either *Riffrost* or *Naara*. Taggart, did either of those cultures claim this region of space in their times?"

Kaitlin nodded. She remembered that ambitious Gunnery Officer who had first come aboard *Marrakesh* intent on being part of the war and a little upset that he'd been assigned to a Tactical Transport instead of a Line Cruiser.

To measure Maddox Nevin then against the young man seated across from her brought a smile to Kaitlin's face. Padraig was turning Maddox into another future captain like himself.

And it would be good.

"Scanning," Nyssa replied as a verbal placeholder. "*Riffrost* shows their outer line a little beyond Sabahattin, but I show no evidence in my records that they ever made it this far. Most of their time was spent facing those proverbial swamps where *A'Zedi* would rise later, holding a front line against what would become the *Holy Imperium of Copez* when *Naara* finally broke apart. Nobody has anything more recent, understanding that we are not privy to most records from *Wronlori* or *Traisa*."

Kaitlin approved there, as well. Smart young woman. She'd go far in whatever field she chose, **and** had been given the gift of Padraig as her first commanding officer, through which lens she would judge the rest.

She turned to Nicodemus. He seemed to be breathing heavily.

"It is possible," he admitted. "Derrik Leath has spent his

career looking for intelligent, alien life forms, but has produced nothing more than evidence of a hundred pranks others have staged. Footprint casts. Blurry images obviously manufactured. Those sorts of things. No DNA. No technology. I would hesitate bringing him into this conversation until we knew for certain. And even then, I would exercise caution, as his motives might lean more towards *prurient curiosity* than science."

Kaitlin scowled at the term, but supposed that one like Leath might be more interested in fucking something utterly exotic, and that sort of thing had gotten him ostracized from polite society. Better than some of the alternatives.

Then everyone was looking at her. Because she was in charge until Padraig took that mantle onto his own shoulders. Kaitlin drew a deep breath and considered the various legalisms that Dimitriou had explained. The purposes of both Padraig and Nicodemus. Even Maddox's new mission to become more than he'd ever imagined he might enjoy.

It came down to her.

"Nicodemus, you will continue with your dig, but we will make it a point to improve your security," she began. "Padraig, I would appreciate a few more armed sailors and some better sensor gear down here to expand our safety range."

Both nodded. She turned and focused on Maddox.

"I need you to act like a Survey Corps officer, Armiger Nevin," she continued, pronouncing a certain kind of doom on the young man and waiting for him to nod. "You will organize a ground force to search out whatever it was that was in the dig area last night. You will investigate it thoroughly. You will attempt First Contact if they are intelligent and you can determine that such a task can be handled safely. Or you will back away if it cannot, at which point we will determine our options."

Nicodemus started to speak and she speared him with a glare that brought the tall man to utter silence.

"We may remain and dig," she offered. "If, however, this is an inhabited world, we are bound by interstellar law and a variety of treaty agreements with the likes of *Wronlori*, *Traisa*, and *Copez*. I will presume that such extends to any intelligent natives of this world until such time as we can contact the correct authorities on Horwin and ask for sharper clarity. Proceed with caution, but you may have just stepped over a line from being an exoarchaeologist to being a grave robber, Professor. Let that thought frame your actions, because I have no doubts that this mission has just gone well beyond what the folks back home originally expected. Questions?"

There were none. She had taken Dimitriou's words and drawn a very bright line for everyone to follow. And they might all end up facing court martials later. Even Nicodemus, because this was a military contract, regardless of who was actually paying, so he came under military law.

And interstellar treaties. A man that smart would understand what that meant, even if folks like Gary Renshaw or Myra Thurston were a bit clueless on those sorts of topics.

Kaitlin drew a deep breath and nodded to Maddox first, then Padraig on the screen.

This mission had indeed just gotten much more interesting.

27

———

Maddox hadn't slowed down. Had, in fact, sucked down extra coffee, loaded with sugar and cream, just because he wasn't sure what the day would bring and figured he should front-load on energy.

They had filled up backpacks with field gear, assuming the possibility of an overnight hike into unknown terrain. He'd let Murphy and Farrell handle that, because they were trained specifically for those tasks. His job was to be the officer in charge of the experts.

The sun was finally rising, but he felt like he'd been going for twelve hours already. Fortunately, he was young, understanding that he could push harder and farther at twenty-seven than he'd be able to in another decade.

And Stevedore Lynch had been correct that he needed to handle this, because the civilians were all wrong. In fact, he'd ordered them all to remain with the dig, unwilling to trust someone untrained in the field when things might get hostile.

His sailors had all been there. With him. Many going back to that damned Leviathan *Sundering Wrath*.

They'd all go to the wall if he needed it.

Hopefully, nobody would.

Maddox paused as the first edge of the local sun appeared, like a bell sounding in his head.

Survey Corps. They went farther out than anybody else.

First in the Field. Even a ship like *Northwind* that *Marrakesh* had rescued had only been a spy ship slipping into *Wronlori* space to investigate a future base that might threaten *A'Zedi*'s inner frontier of expansion.

Survey Corps was the tip of the spear, but not necessarily a spear. Not every problem was a military one.

That did not, however, prevent him from bringing along Trinh Hoàng and her Light Disruptor Cannon. Or Riley Erson, who was usually a field medic assigned to Dr. Hyden on the ship, but who also spent her time in security.

Murphy was on point as they started the walk out to the dig. *Roadrunner* had brought a hand-held scanner that Hoàng had in her hands, ready to be dropped if she needed to draw a pistol or bring down a small castle.

Maddox's team led, with Farrell bringing the others, separated by a gap of forty meters. *Roadrunner* had also brought down six more people to fill in security gaps until they knew what to expect from Sabahattin.

His job. Right here. Right now. On point.

The walk didn't take long. There was already a well-worn path, in spite of this being just their third day planetside. It would become a road at some point. Maybe the start of a city, depending, if there really was an ancient starport under this turf, just waiting for heavy equipment to scrape down to that old surface.

Fleet would be interested. Locals might not be. And it was their world, so they got to decide things. Lucky for them that it had been an *A'Zedi* mission. *Wronlori* wouldn't ask. *Traisa* had strong fascist leanings not far below the surface, with the most powerful seizing ultimate power as Supreme Autocrat, the whole having overthrown their kings and executed everyone with royal blood to make a point a century ago.

They wouldn't ask the locals nicely, either.

That was Maddox's job.

"Murphy, what do you have?" Maddox asked as they got to the dig itself, noting that the tarps didn't appear to have been disturbed.

That, or they'd been put back.

Mark of intelligence, or predators sniffing and not finding food worth digging?

Too early to say.

Farrell had held her team back at the edge of the flight line, off to one side where she could see around back better.

"I've got a mess of footprints, sir," Murphy said, kneeling down while Hoàng stood close by and ignored the ground to watch the horizon. "Our civilians don't have a military tread, so it's hard to distinguish."

"Understood," Maddox replied. "Scout team, shift forward and down the back so Murphy can look for tracks."

He turned to Farrell and waved her people closer, waiting on the high point until she joined him.

"This is yours," he said, pointing at the mound under their feet. "We're looking over there and will stay in touch via comm with both you and the ship."

"Good luck, sir," she said, shifting to stand like a war goddess statue as the others started inspecting their gear.

Maddox hadn't seen anything moved or broken, but he wasn't touching things, either.

Simply moving on.

They'd explored back here, mostly just walking circles, but there wasn't much to see. More rolling plains slowly descending as you kept going east, the plateau dropping a bit sharply down to a coastal plain that wasn't very wide. On the left, it actually went up some, with a range of hills where it looked like enough rain fell to support trees.

In the distance, there were even mountains, but nobody had looked all that closely over there, because people tended to want to live in less challenging circumstances when they could.

Murphy meandered. Hoàng watched her screens. Maddox and the rest watched the grass in case anything jumped up suddenly.

"Sir, I might have something," Murphy announced, gesturing.

Maddox moved closer, but nothing was obvious.

"Footprints, sir," he said. "Guessing a moccasin sort of thing instead of treads and heels. Looks human enough, within limits. Heads that way."

He pointed and Maddox looked up. Towards the hills? Back in the forest? Mountain?

"Any other creature signs?" Maddox asked.

"Been looking, sir," Murphy replied. "Nothing obvious, but this terrain won't hold trail well. Doubly so if it is artificial. Might be more if we got into the trees."

Why trees?

Maddox didn't didn't know, but he understood that he had a mission, so he drew out his comm and activated it.

"Scout Team Nevin," he announced, knowing it would be recorded up on the ship in case something happened. "Headed a little west of north from the dig site. Specialist Murphy has located what might be tracks and a trail, origin unknown at present. We'll check in every hour or so as we go."

"Good luck, Nevin," Captain Boru replied, so Maddox felt better.

If something happened to him, he had *Marrakesh* backing him up.

Or avenging him, if it came to that.

28

———

Nicodemus took extra time this morning as they uncovered the hole that Nevin and Yves had so laboriously created for him yesterday.

Someone or something had touched it. Disturbed it.

Had they stolen anything?

"Gary, join me," he said, again drawing the small man along.

Who knew? If Gary invented new sensors that *A'Zedi* could use, would that make exoarchaeology easier? And maybe Gary would get the next grant and need some assistance?

Always plan ahead.

The space below looked normal enough. No sudden gaps in the hull indicating a break-in. No surprises.

And Armiger Nevin was off tracking whoever had done it, while Cameron Farrell held watch closer, smoldering with an obvious anger and looking for a target upon which to unleash it.

"What do you think, Nicodemus?" Gary asked. "Aft or lateral?"

It was a cogent question. The top was generally flat, only rounded out on the edges. No hatch was immediately obvious, but not everyone centered them, either. And he needed to access the interior to know the truth of the thing.

He measured with his mind, then looked up at Yves, already holding a shovel and smiling.

"Let us work this hole forward just enough that two diggers can work simultaneously," Nicodemus decided. "Then we will go laterally until we find a hatch. If we clear more than six meters of width, we'll stop and work aft, clearing as many of the top layers as we can until we find something that can identify the wreck better."

Yves nodded and held out a hand, pulling Nicodemus out of the hole and hopping in with Gary, the two of them actually able to work well in the confined space. Kaitlin hadn't joined him today, remaining at the base camp in order to coordinate things, so he grabbed Benton and brought her close.

"Your thoughts?" he asked.

The woman was closer to being an intellectual equal than any of the other civilians he had brought, save perhaps Gary.

"Obviously, you were expecting a hatch on top for emergency access," she replied as she stepped close enough to make the conversation private. "Are we more likely to find a loading hatch to port or starboard, historically?"

He paused to consider that, realizing that he might be the only starship engineering expert on the surface, not counting some of the sailors he didn't know at all.

"A smart navy builds them on both sides," he replied. "Generally at about the same point aft from the bridge, so that supplies can be located near the big engineering spaces."

"Would it be worth cutting down a side and working laterally, in the same manner as the boys are doing?" she pressed.

Nicodemus turned and visualized a freighter as *Riffrost* had built them in the early days. Not that much different from late *Naara* designs, because the physics hadn't changed at all and the aesthetics were constrained by the need to land in an atmosphere.

He did note a bit of a flare in the lump. Possibly stubby wings or aerofoils. Alternatively, how the wind had deposited blown soil and detritus.

Nicodemus paced it off in his mind, then walked to a spot about ten meters forward from where Gary and Yves were working.

"Here, probably," he told her, as Benton had trailed silently along.

"Do we care all that much about side dirt?" she asked.

"We do not," he shook his head. "But put it through a metal detector anyway, just in case. That will speed the task. You were thinking of using the new crane?"

"I was, but wasn't sure how you would utilize it," she replied..

Looking at the layout, he suddenly saw the shape of what he wanted to create.

"Madame Farrell," he called to get her attention. "I would like your thoughts on assembling the crane here, then using it to clear the sides of the hill until we hit metal, dumping the soil there."

Something in her eyes lit up in a manner that was almost frightening, but Nicodemus held his ground.

"I think that would be an exceptional idea, Professor," she said, then looked around. "Gold team, shift to assembling the tower and get it operational. Priority."

Nicodemus watched about half of the security folks suddenly drop what they were doing to shift gears, moving to the pile of light beams that had been created in order to be assembled quickly and by hand, using nothing more than muscle and hand-held tools. All currently in the flatbed of a cargorunner that had been intended to set up another square of fence today.

In almost no time, a derrick came into being, some four meters wide at the bottom, tapering to a two-meter platform and a series of pulleys for a winch. The whole was attached to the wheeled cart with the winch itself at one end and anchors that could be driven into the soil to hold the unit stable.

Cables got strung and tested. A bucket was added, roughly a meter wide and half that deep, with teeth and an edge designed to bite into soil.

Farrell took her space atop the thing, walking a slow square from some twenty meters elevation, letting her potentially see everything she needed.

A small woman with Asian features presented herself when the unit was ready.

"Yua Kaneko, Professor," she introduced herself. "Where would you like the first bite?"

Aggressive. All of them were, as if they wanted to clear this wreck as much as he did. Maybe more, if that was possible.

Did they feel the sands sliding through that hourglass like he did?

"Here," Nicodemus told her. "I presume the sides are squarish, while the hill tapers from accumulated silt, so I'm not entirely certain how deep it is until we remove several layers."

"I'd say roughly fifty centimeters at the top, Professor," she smiled. "Closer to four meters at the bottom."

He blinked at her.

"Civil engineering is part of the curriculum, sir," she offered, then gestured him to move out of the way. "Cutting team, stand by for the bucket!"

Nicodemus watched mesmerized as Kaneko set the bucket with the help of the sailor on the winch and Farrell spotting from above. The first slice wasn't that deep, ripping off grass and roots to expose a rich, deep soil beneath that had a homey smell that always reminded him of archaeological digs.

Dirt, newly exposed and drying, had a particular scent that got deep in his brain.

Above, Gary and Yves continued to work, but already Nicodemus could see how this crane could be used to scrape away a lot of soil quickly, in order to get at the valuable materials underneath.

And, truth be told, this was less about proper archaeology, where you studied the contents of every single bucket for the slightest trace of history, and more about exposing a buried starship so that he could see what was there.

And prove a couple of people wrong. He'd have to sneak a letter back to his old faculty competition, but it could be done.

No coordinates. Just images that Myra Thurston was taking in her job as Dig Photographer.

And a few, not-so-subtle taunts. It wasn't like they didn't have it coming, after all.

Later. Right now, that bucket was handling days of tedious labor in minutes.

This was what he could accomplish with enough funds. Next time, he would need a skid-loader or a small agricultural tractor with some digging implements.

Soon, he would see a starship, visible for the first time in centuries.

29

Nyssa had been writing all manner of new code to analyze the data she had vacuumed up on the flight out. Tools that should have been included but weren't because most folks like her worked on Horwin, in little cubicles.

She was on the front lines, literally.

Today, she was on the Bridge working, with Glen and Bex both on duty doing things that let her not pay as close attention as she normally would.

Her screen beeped.

"Taggart," Nyssa said. "What have you got, Glen?"

"Maybe an inbound ship, sir," Glen said. "Sending you the signal now."

Nyssa automatically saved her work and minimized that screen as she brought up Glen's feed.

Yes, something. Clear out on the edge of her Aetherial Scanners, but not headed directly at them. Running laterally and curling in a bit, but at a distance of around eight light-years. Moving slowly, too, but as she watched, the signal suddenly turned sharply towards her.

And accelerated.

She felt like a tuna that had suddenly been spotted by a shark.

Nyssa checked her other screens, but *Marrakesh* and the inbound were the only vessels currently visible.

Still, someone had seen them. And accelerated from Mark Two to Mark Five in response. The updated estimated time to interception was now eighty minutes.

Nyssa considered her options. And Captain Boru's standing orders for operations this far from home and support.

She nodded to herself, then reached over and opened the rocker switch to reveal a button underneath. Simultaneously, she opened the ship-wide intercom and pushed it.

"All hands to action stations," Nyssa announced as the alarms started up. "Unknown vessel closing at a high rate of speed, intentions unknown. Stand by for potential combat operations."

30

Padraig had been doing paperwork, having just eaten a late lunch. The alert had him sprinting forward and dodging other crew members racing to their own stations.

Nyssa Taggart had the Bridge, but Zarah Halloran was only two steps behind Padraig, and Gunner Tindal was already in Maddox Nevin's station, live and awaiting orders as he slammed into his seat.

"Main screen," Padraig called.

Immediately, the image of the scan zone came up, showing *Marrakesh* and Sabahattin at the center, with a single ping closing on a direct line. No others, but someone was racing inwards, instead of sailing politely along or turning away.

"Any idea who they are?" he asked Nyssa.

"Negative, sir," she replied. "Prior behavior suggested that they were patrolling, then spotted us and immediately turned to engage. They are not close enough to identify or hail."

Padraig wanted to curse, but held it in. The absolute worst possible time for someone to come along, because the folks on the ground risked being abandoned if *Marrakesh* was chased off, or had to abandon their dig just at the moment when things on the ground had gotten interesting.

And the longer he waited, the riskier the situation got.

He dialed a number.

"Base camp. Lynch."

"Kaitlin, it's Padraig," he said. "We have an inbound vessel closing at high speed. They will arrive in about sixty minutes, give or take. Intentions unknown. Identity unknown."

"Should we evacuate?" she asked, turning sharp. "Maddox is out in the field, but we can pick him up with *Crime Lab* on the way to orbit."

Padraig nodded to himself. *Marrakesh* was a Tactical Transport. Cruiser size, but only frigate firepower if there was trouble. And his best Gunner was down on the ground, though Tindal was no slouch at that sort of thing and Padraig still knew how to fight a starship if he had to.

"Stand by," he said, then turned. "Radio, confirm only one signal?"

"Affirmative, Captain," she replied. "One vessel only, and I have not picked up any Aetherial signals that might be them calling for assistance. Patrol vessel?"

"That or a pirate," Padraig agreed. "Which probably means smaller and in for a bit of a surprise shortly. Kaitlin, did you catch all that?"

"I did, Padraig," she said. "We should be safe enough down here, if you need to chase someone off?"

"Yes, but stay alert in case we do need to pull everybody up, should that turn out to be a scout calling for a squadron to evict us," he said.

"Understood," she replied. "I'll let Maddox know."

"*Marrakesh* out."

He cut the line and looked around.

"We'll assume that they'll drop out ready to fight, but we won't fire first, Tindal," he said. "Radio, prepare a package to be transmitted to Fleet and try to keep the signal narrow enough that we don't tell everyone that there's a ship out here. Everybody take bio-breaks and do whatever else you need, I want you ready in twenty minutes. Questions?"

Everyone shook their heads. Now was the hard part, waiting for a ship to close, but Nyssa and her team had caught them clear at the edge of scanner range, so he had time to prepare. For what, he didn't know, but he had the right crew to handle it.

Shortly, they would.

31

Maddox kept the group close together as they walked, mostly because Hoàng could scan a reasonable distance ahead in case someone was hiding in ambush, and he didn't want folks wandering outside that range.

Murphy had made pretty good time, once he decided that the folks had moved in a pretty straight line towards the closest copse of trees. The ground was starting to slope uphill, but not sharp or anything. Rising plains where tectonics had wrinkled things to throw up those mountains ahead of him. Forests covering things in such a way that it almost made things look black, except where the morning fog hadn't burned off yet.

Beautiful countryside. Raw nature, though it had probably been inhabited at some point.

And might still be. Wouldn't know until they got to wherever it was they were going.

By mid-day, they had crossed all the grasslands and were getting deeper into the forest itself. Maybe a hundred meters elevation above the dig, looking back and down into the flatlands behind them.

"Murphy, you still have their trail?" Maddox asked.

"Aye, sir," the sailor replied. "Getting a little easier. Think they were in a hurry, because their trailcraft was breaking down at this point and I can confirm two sets of tracks. Small feet in leather moccasins."

"How small?" he asked.

"Female with small feet, if we're talking adult humans, sir," Murphy said. "Hoàng-sized, maybe. Light and moving at a pretty good clip."

"Like maybe we spooked them?" Maddox asked.

"Somebody did, sir," Murphy said. "Same time, these tracks are only a couple of hours old, so they passed here about the time we were hitting the dig. At or just after dawn."

"Huh," Maddox grunted. "Hoàng, see anything ahead of us?"

He watched her adjust the scanner and point it ahead, shifting left to right slowly like taking a panorama with a camera.

"There are a lot of animals in there," she replied. "Some big, some small. Scanner is mostly throwing what look like false positives, bouncing silly off trees. Want me to keep doing the forward scan or go back to perimeter, sir?"

"Forward. We're safe enough for now," he decided. "Murphy, any way you can pick up the pace?"

"Easy enough, sir," the man nodded. "Two people jogging instead of moving cautiously originally. Except that it looks like they got to the trees and slowed way down. Like they were feeling safe."

"Don't get us ambushed, but keep up if we can," Maddox replied. "Catch them, if possible."

He started to say more when his comm chirped.

"Nevin."

"It's Lynch," the Stevedore said. "Captain has just picked up a signal indicating an inbound vessel approaching *Marrakesh*."

"Do we abort our pursuit, sir?" he asked. "Murphy has identified tracks of two people that we are pursuing, but we are also going deeper into the forest at present, and evac will be more difficult if we insert."

"You continue on for now, Nevin," she ordered. "We may

send *Crime Lab* over to get you, once we know the situation in orbit, but Padraig is aiming for diplomacy first, then a hard bluff second. If the latter and it works, we'll likely be abandoning Sabahattin for the time being."

"Understood, sir," Maddox replied. "We'll stay sharp here."

"Stay safe first, Armiger," she ordered, then cut the line.

Maddox looked at his people and caught their nods. The disappointment that whoever they had been pursuing might get away at this point, due to circumstances beyond anybody's control.

Then he smiled at them.

"Hoàng, set your scanner to hard forward," he ordered. "Everybody else watch the flanks. Murphy, I'd like to run them down if you can, just so we can know who it is. They might not want to stay and talk, but if we can get images, at least we'll have a starting point. Go."

And they were off, somewhat quicker than a jog, maybe closer to a lope, minus the whooping with excitement he could see in their faces.

Risk, but that was life in the Survey Corps. Just a different kind.

32

Nicodemus was absolutely buying an excavator when he got home, however he had to do it and even if he had to trade for a bigger shuttle and strip *Crime Lab* bare to haul everything.

In half a day, they had exposed twenty meters of the ship's flank. Gary and Yves had been pulled off the top, once it was obvious that the crane could remove things so much faster. Not a lot of metal debris when the contents were dumped, but that was in line with Nicodemus's expectation that the ships had been abandoned until they got buried by leaves and dirt.

Farrell descending from her tower at breakneck speed caused him to pull up short and watch. She was coming to him. Jogging. He'd heard some conversation over the comm, but hadn't been paying attention.

That might have been a mistake.

"Sir, we have a situation," she said as she skidded to a halt. "*Marrakesh* has detected an inbound vessel, closing at a high rate of speed indicating an intercept. We've been notified to stand ready for emergency evacuation."

Nicodemus couldn't help himself. To come this far. To know that he'd been right. And to have to run at the moment of his triumph? He didn't think a sailor like Farrell would learn any new vocabulary as he cursed the gods, his fate, and whoever else might be in range. Finally, he settled. Studied the woman closely. Noted the muscles.

"How many people can we get aboard *Crime Lab* in a pinch?" he asked her.

"Short hop to orbit, sir?" she asked. "Everybody. However, the Stevedore wants us to hold *Crime Lab* ready to extract Armiger Nevin's team, possibly from hostile terrain."

More cursing. Then he had an idea.

"How quickly could your sailors make the run to the shuttle at the camp?" he asked. "Assuming we put my people on *Crime Lab*, plus whoever is flying it, could you get there fast enough to escape while we went after Nevin?"

He liked that boy. Maddox Nevin had possibly altered the course of Gary Renshaw's life. And asked a lot of interested and useful questions, when Nicodemus was used to sly derision from most folks.

Maddox would be rescued.

"I can pull a chunk of my people out right now, sir," she replied. "Stage both camps into a temporary shutdown, in case we're running for our lives. Means folks are eating cold sand-wiches for dinner, but we can be ready to launch fast. I'll stay put handling security and Kaneko can fly the shuttle."

"How soon will we know, one way or the other?" he asked her.

"Under an hour," Farrell said.

"Do what you need to do, then," he said. "We'll work right up to the whistle."

She turned away and started issuing orders to her people.

Nicodemus went to explain what was going on to the other civilians.

33

———

Padraig was settled in. Ready for action. Pain in the ass to have to do it here. Especially today. Not his call. Nothing he could do but stand by.

"Radio, time to intercept?" he called.

"Two minutes," she replied. "Depending on how close they come out of Ghost-space."

"Helm, begin acceleration," Padraig ordered. "Head us out and over the north pole, ready to come about and slingshot one way or the other once we know what we're facing. Particle cannon and railgun pulsar teams stand ready to engage incoming missiles if they decide to shoot first. Gunner, hold your missiles for now. What have you got loaded?"

"Standard array, sir," Tindal replied instantly. "Gunnery Officer Nevin generally keeps two Sixes and four Nines loaded, on the theory that we usually need to distract someone while we run."

"Excellent, Guns," Padraig said. "Keep that mix if we end up launching, until I tell you otherwise."

Big missiles. They got launched sideways using steam catapults, then rotated on internal gyroscopes, located their target, and lit their engines. At burnout speed, they separated into component parts, spreading out like a shotgun blast, because a solid hunk of steel alloy at one percent lightspeed had a hell of a lot of boom to it. Adding any nuclear explosives would hardly change the resulting violence.

Threes, Sixes, and Nines, indicating the number of fragments they split into. Some ships carried Twelves, but those were more for saturation bombardment. Or attacking swarms of patrol craft too small for Ghostdrives.

Hopefully, there'd be no firing today, and someone wanted to chat. Or warn him off, in which case they might start with diplomacy.

And maybe end there.

He had some coffee in a sippy cup, just so he could stay focused. And it gave him time to stop and drink if he was on screen talking to someone. Casual was a way of forcing things to calm down.

Useful, with people still on the ground.

"Radio, call the cadence," he ordered.

"Twenty seconds to contact," she replied. "Ten seconds. All hands, stand by."

The other ship dropped out of Ghost-space and appeared. Not all that close, either, which meant that they were investigating rather than attacking without provocation. Screens showed them about on the solar ecliptic, which was expected if they planned to insert into a normal orbit.

"Scan them, Taggart," Padraig ordered. "And send a friendly hail to see how they want to play this."

"Captain, I'm getting *Traisa* colors," she said. "Vessel identifies as the Patrol Scout *Baldur Schreiber*. Datacore says light destroyer design."

"A patrol scout isn't a match for *Marrakesh* for firepower," Padraig told her. "Keep a watch on him and continue hail. Helm, stand by to close if he wants trouble, but hold for my order. Guns, same."

"Aye, sir," they replied.

Padraig waited. *Baldur Schreiber* would need a moment to locate him, since *Marrakesh* had shifted. And that vessel had probably homed in on the probe in orbit, since it would be visible at that range. Maybe they'd found the others and tracked this direction to see if *Wronlori* was up to no good?

Traisa was neutral in the current War of the Fourth Alliance, *A'Zedi* and *Copez* against *Wronlori*. didn't mean much, this far from home, though. And they'd found *Wronlori* last time around.

"Captain, I'm getting a hail from *Baldur Schreiber*," Nyssa said.

"Main screen," he ordered.

The panel lit up, showing a tall blondish man. Pale, like *Traisans* tended to be, much more like *Wronlori* than *A'Zedi's* darker features. Captain's tabs on his shoulders. Rugged face with a well-trimmed beard turning gray, though the rest of his hair was still a softly faded blond. Rather attractive, even.

"Captain Padraig Boru, *A'Zedi* Tactical Transport *Marrakesh*, Captain. To whom do I have the pleasure of speaking?"

It took the man a moment to compose himself, his initial scowl giving way to a neutral smile.

"Captain Dennis Gerhardt," the man replied. "You are a long ways from home, *Marrakesh*."

Padraig nodded and relaxed a notch. Hopefully, they could talk. *Baldur Schreiber* was probably expecting to run into a pirate. Or a *Wronlori* vessel building a forward base from which they might slip around behind *Traisa's* front lines for the same sort of surprise attack as they'd thrown at *A'Zedi* at Eworn almost four years ago.

"Conducting an exoarchaeological expedition, *Baldur Schreiber*," Padraig countered. "Unclaimed space, as far as we've been able to identify to date."

He left it at that, mostly to see if Gerhardt would claim otherwise.

"Exoarchaeology, *Marrakesh*?" Gerhardt asked, features puzzled now. "Here?"

"Indeed, Captain," Padraig nodded. "Our records show that it was previously inhabited, and my Fleet sent *Marrakesh* because we could haul enough supplies to spend a few months digging to confirm some of what we've already found on the ground. No intention to build a base here at the moment."

Padraig paused there, smiling. He didn't need to mention that they'd been here less than a week. Or that the world might yet have human inhabitants. An *A'Zedi* dig would claim precedence unless *Traisa* had inserted their own base or operation prior, and Nyssa had specifically looked for such things.

And not found it.

The natives could come up later, once Maddox knew what he was chasing, and might change all equations again.

"Inhabited, Captain Boru?" Gerhardt scoffed. "I find that hard to believe."

"If you'd like to send a team over, Captain Gerhardt, I was in the process of preparing to send some supplies to the ground this afternoon. I'd be happy to transport some observers from *Baldur Schreiber* to show you what we've been up to."

As in, neutral, diplomatic folks like say, your First Officer or someone important enough to be believed, but not a combat team. I have people on the ground already handling those tasks.

Again, not exactly lies, but not entirely truths, either. Diplomatic evasions. Padraig was pretty good at that sort of thing.

"Stand by," Gerhardt said suddenly, and the screen froze.

Probably his own Legal Affairs Officer or Exec leaning in to whisper something. Possibly explaining that *Marrakesh* had primacy of claim at the moment. Might not stand up in a court of law, but then again, it might.

And Padraig had a duty to the natives, whoever they were, to protect them from *Traisa* suddenly deciding to expand and colonize this direction. Even *Traisa* wouldn't pick a fight with *A'Zedi*. Not without a better reason than an archaeological expedition.

Not unless Padraig's people found something galaxy-shattering.

Did a new human world count? True aliens would upend everything and everyone, even if they were still Iron Age or lower on the scale.

Nobody had ever found any evidence of any higher life forms besides humans.

The screen flickered to life again.

"I have just spoken with my senior staff, Captain Boru," Captain Gerhardt said. "We would like to take you up on the offer of an observer mission."

Padraig nodded. They were going to call his bluff, but he wasn't exactly bluffing. Shading the truth a bit, but not much.

"Two officers and a couple of enlisted sailors, Captain Gerhardt?" Padraig volleyed. "I'd ask that they not be armed, but feel free to bring electronics to record things. And they can talk to you from the surface."

"How soon, Captain Boru?" Gerhardt asked.

"As soon as we can return to our original orbital path and rendezvous with your shuttle, Captain Gerhardt," Padraig said. "We'll have a quick briefing here with comm lines open, then send my shuttle down with supplies."

"Very good, Captain Boru," the man nodded. "We'll be along shortly."

Padraig cut the line and dialed aft.

"Flight Deck. Rafferty."

"Air Boss, load *Roadrunner* up with supplies as quickly as you can," Padraig ordered. "Then stand by for a *Traisan* shuttle to dock in your bay to deliver some folks."

"Understood, sir," the man said. "In process."

Padraig cut the line and leaned back a moment before he activated the ship-wide.

"All hands, stand down a little," he announced. "The *Traisan* vessel appears friendly and we'll be hosting some guests, but don't relax entirely just yet. Captain out."

34

Kaitlin nodded when Padraig finished his explanation. Probably about as good an outcome as they could expect at present. Not as good as being entirely missed. Not as bad as open warfare overhead.

She started to call Cam, then thought better of it and walked over to the dig instead. It wasn't that far, and she needed to burn off some of her nervous energy.

Cam and Nicodemus both met her at the edge of the camp.

"There will be some *Traisan* officers visiting shortly," she told them. "Padraig invited them to observe and they accepted. We'll host them on the ground at least overnight, then determine our plans. Captain Boru did not mention Maddox's secondary mission, so we'll leave that part out for now and the captains can sort it out later."

"We can keep digging?" Nicodemus asked. It was really all he cared about.

"You can," she assured him. "I came to see what progress you've made, because even with binoculars it is hard to tell from over there."

"Come," he said, gesturing.

Cam nodded and turned away, returning to her tower where she could keep watch on the entire valley floor.

Yua Kaneko was practically covered in dirt. And appeared to be cackling with laughter. Kaitlin could see why, given that they had managed to uncover a significant portion of the ship's hull enough that folks were using brooms to sweep dirt away.

As with yesterday, the hull metal color struck her. Lighter than she was used to. Almost silver, instead of the deep gray that marked most modern vessels.

"Found it," Benton announced as they got close.

Nicodemus gave a cry.

"Show me!" he demanded.

They ended up at the edge of the gouge, where dirt had been cleared and the hull was visible on the side. Outlines of a hatch or an airlock, clearly visible mostly from the way dirt had been packed into the seams and several folks were carefully working with chisels or butter knives to clear them.

"Do we know what it is yet?" Kaitlin asked as they trooped close and inspected things.

"The lines suggest an extremely early *Riffrost* design," Nicodemus replied. "*Naara* would have used a different alloy with a more golden hue that made their ships utterly brilliant in the sun. *Riffrost* went more silver, eventually leading to the darker colors everyone employs today."

"Wondered about that," Kaitlin nodded.

"The shape and the location suggest a medium-sized cargo vessel," he continued. "More boxy than the warships of that era, where there was a tendency to streamline things like knives."

"Will you be able to open it?" Kaitlin asked. "That is, short of destroying things to get in?"

"Gary, what do you have?" Nicodemus asked.

"It looks like a standard manual override," Gary replied from where he was stretched out flat on his stomach inspecting the bottom of the hatch. "Almost like what we use today."

"That would not surprise me, Gary," Kaitlin called. "Things

like that become standards that live for a very long time, once people trust them. Engineers are extremely cautious about changing things that work."

"Then I'll need a power torque with a multi-pin head and some lubricant to get into the wheel itself," Gary said. "Then more lubricant on the wheel and we might be able to open this ship up."

Kaitlin turned to Nicodemus and got serious. His smile damped down quickly and he calmed.

"I might recommend that we wait until our guests arrive from orbit," Kaitlin offered in a serious voice. "That way we are properly conducting exoarchaeology, so that they can witness it themselves. Padraig has impressed on them the academic side of this mission, and I'd like to reinforce that."

"Do you think that is wise?" he asked quietly.

"I do," she nodded. "After all, if they decide to, they can easily keep *A'Zedi* vessels away, given the sailing distances involved, and I doubt that your find currently rises to the level where *A'Zedi* will wish to station an entire squadron or fleet out here permanently to claim this system. Let us seduce *Traisa* into assisting."

He considered it, then nodded.

"Yes, probably for the best," Nicodemus said, then turned and clapped his hands. "Everyone! We will take a long break at this point, returning to camp to eat and relax, then bringing our new guests out when they arrive, so that we can show off."

Groans and the usual bitching, but twenty minutes ago they had all been prepared to run for their lives to board a shuttle.

And Padraig seemed to have things in hand in orbit. It would be her job to handle them down here.

35

Maddox was a little winded, but so were the rest of his sailors and he didn't feel so bad. Still, he could see spending more time on the treadmill starting next week. And maybe fewer desserts in his future.

Getting ready for the next stage of his life. Hadn't both Captain and Radio called this mission something of a crossroads?

His as well, it seemed.

A beep drew his attention.

"I've got something," Trinh gasped. "Multiple thermal and audio signals on this vector, left about twenty degrees."

"Hill slopes up that way," Murphy replied, a little less winded than the rest but still breathing heavily. "Cliff faces, I would have thought, though. Unless they have a pass or maybe a cave."

Maddox started to reply when a scream ripped the afternoon in two. High. Ugly. Terror.

The kind of shit that froze your blood.

"Someone's in trouble," he decided, listening to his gut. "Draw arms and double time. *Move it, sailors.*"

Maddox didn't wait for the others. Instead, he started running, trusting his feet to find smooth terrain and keeping his eyes and Adjustable Disruptor up as he moved. Behind him, stomping announced the rest of his sailors, but his job was to lead.

He led.

The slope was heavy with trees overhead that cut out light, so he was mostly jogging uphill over pine needles and downed branches, rather than having to deal with brush.

That cry sounded again, except that this time it was more triumphant, like a predator that has brought his prey down and is calling the rest of the pack to feed.

Maddox had no idea what sorts of things lived in Sabahattin's forests, but he was an officer.

He ran as fast he could.

Movement caused him to veer a little more to his left as he came around some trees, right to the edge of a clearing maybe twenty-five meters across. Like Murphy had said, cliff faces in this direction, but he didn't see a cave or a ladder.

Instead, he saw a pair of humanoid figures backed up against the vertical rock wall, with some big monster in gray fur threatening them. Quadruped. Cat-like, but maybe four hundred kilos of muscle and rage, growling at the two figures.

Maddox had an instant to see that one of the two was down on their butt, leaning against the rock face and holding a spear outward, while the other stood over them defensively.

Then the big, gray cat turned a face filled with huge eyes and lots of teeth to growl at Maddox.

Warning him off? Maddox didn't know. It coiled up like it was about to pounce on him, so Maddox shot it. Trinh's legs must have been churning like a duck's to keep up because she was suddenly beside him, also firing, except that she'd taken the time to pull the Light Disruptor Cannon off her back and was firing it from a hip like some action vid star.

Big cat got blasted ass over teakettle across the clearing, tumbling several times and smoking.

Sure as shit dead, because one of those bolts had missed and blown apart a tree thicker than Maddox's waist. Thankfully, it fell away from anyone.

More sailors arrived, but the cat was done.

Maddox turned his attention to the two figures backed up to the wall and trapped there by whatever the hell that thing had been.

The standing one had a spear pointed at him, but they weren't getting any closer.

He looked closer and guessed that he was looking at a teenage girl. She looked a lot like his sister Noelle had at that age, only a lot paler.

Then she spoke.

36

———————

Padraig waited until the flight bay signaled safe, then followed Walt Rafferty through the airlock hatch. The *Traisan* shuttle was just opening up as they got close and two officers descended the ramp.

"Commander," he nodded to the woman in charge.

"Maja Huffmann, Captain Boru," she replied, standing tall and square in front of him. "First Officer of *Baldur Schreiber*."

Not quite at attention, but a bit more formal than he would have preferred.

Padraig took a moment to study her.

Tall, blonde, muscular, and tough-looking. Probably attractive physically, but Padraig really wasn't that into women and something about her demeanor put him off. The Lieutenant next to her gave the impression of a legal affairs officer like Nektaria Dimitriou, but more gray and backgroundy, if he could say that without insulting the man. Also not that attractive.

"Lt. Schmidt," Commander Huff introduced the fellow.

A pair of sailors accompanied them, both with packs no doubt loaded for camping. No weapons, but both looked like they knew their way around bar fights.

Padraig idly wished that Cameron Farrell and Trinh Hoàng were here, but he did have Anderson Lorenzen handy, one of the biggest crew members on the ship, and while not the sharpest spoon in the drawer, probably still the toughest.

"Welcome aboard *Marrakesh*," Padraig said to all four. "At present, the plan is to cross-ship you to our other shuttle, clear the bay, and fly to the surface to where my Stevedore is supervising a mixed crew of civilians and sailors on the dig."

"Will you be accompanying us, Captain Boru?" she asked.

"I hadn't planned to, but there is flexibility in my schedule," he said.

Padraig reached for his comm, but it was already chirping.

"Boru," he said simply, wondering who was calling, knowing what was going on.

"Commander Messier, sir," Chance replied, sounding much more formal than usual. "I've just been in touch with the ground, and I think it would be to everyone's benefit if you did take command down there."

Padraig held his breath for a moment, then nodded. Chance knew something and wasn't willing to share with the visitors just yet, or she might have simply used the overhead intercom.

"Excellent, Commander," Padraig said. "You take command here and work with Taggart on her ongoing duties while I travel to the surface with Commander Huffmann."

He turned to Rafferty.

"I'll be joining you, Air Boss," Padraig said.

"Ready to load, sir," Walt replied without any outward emotion.

Again, more serious than normal. Much more serious.

But something was up. Padraig turned to the visitors.

"Commander, if you'd care to join me, we'll be off."

Rafferty led and the others followed, over to where *Roadrunner* had been packed with a variety of boxes that had been staged to be hauled down whenever. Now it made it look like a serious operation, and he grinned that Walt had stepped up so far.

Once aboard, Rafferty was flying, which didn't surprise Padraig one bit. The bay got sealed and evacuated, then the outer door opened and *Roadrunner* followed the *Traisan* shuttle out into space. They were headed home, while *Roadrunner* nosed over and started to dive to the surface.

37

Maddox waved his sailors to remain in place. Trinh had her cannon handy, in case there was trouble, so Maddox went ahead and holstered his pistol.

Definitely a girl. Appeared to be completely human, wearing an outfit that might have been carved off an elk or a moose, with the fur still on. Jacket. Leggings, hat. Some sort of scarf and gloves knitted by hand.

He hadn't understood a word she'd said. Merely a string of syllables ending in an interrogative that his brain wanted to translate as, "Who the hell are you?"

Body language helped.

"I'm Armiger Maddox Nevin," he said calmly, arms out and palms forward in a way he hoped looked peaceful.

Not like she didn't know what his pistol or Trinh's Disruptor Cannon could do, but the girl kept her spear centered on him from about ten meters away.

The other one was doing the same, but sitting on her butt. And favoring one leg, as if she'd twisted a knee or ankle at some point.

Like from running for your life from that dead cat. Maddox glanced over, but it was still smoldering. And not twitching.

The girl replied. Less emotion in her voice. No trust at all.

He took one step forward and paused.

"I'd like to help," he offered.

Her face screwed up in confusion that felt like his, so maybe nobody spoke a common language, in which case he had one hell of a game in front of him to convey anything.

Then he had an idea.

Slowly. Carefully. Deliberately, Maddox pulled out his comm and dialed a number.

"Farrell."

"It's Nevin," he replied. "Is the Professor anywhere close?"

"Stand by," she called. "Yua, catch!"

The sound of a comm being thrown—dropped?—and suddenly Yua Kaneko was there.

"Kaneko."

"I need the Professor," Maddox repeated.

"This is Professor Whitlaw, Armiger," the man said.

"I have a linguistics problem, sir," Maddox said. "Stand by."

Maddox held out the comm to the standing girl.

"I'd like you to say something for the Professor," he said. "Something long and preferably complicated so he has a chance to understand it. I hope I'm making sense."

The girl cocked her head at him, then fired off a couple of long sentences.

Then the Professor answered, causing just about everybody to jump almost out of their skins.

A conversation ensued. Balky. Halting. Both girls perked up at one point and looked directly at him, ignoring the comm.

"Armiger, I'll explain more later, but it appears they are speaking an archaic dialect of *Riffrost*," the Professor switched languages back. "The girl apparently seated injured her leg, and I've told her you have a medic. That's Stavroula. The one standing and protecting her cousin or kinswoman is Sotiria."

"Sotiria," Maddox repeated.

That girl nodded.

"Stavroula?" he looked at the other, noting her nod and the grimace on her face, teeth gritted against pain.

"Maddox," he said, tapping his chest. Then he pointed to his medic. "Riley."

"Maddox. Riley," Sotiria repeated, weirdly accented but understandable.

"Professor, Riley is the medic," Maddox said. "I'd like the two of us to approach the young ladies so we can treat Stavroula. Can you explain?"

More gibberish. Maddox could see some language lessons in his future, if it was a tongue that the Professor understood.

How many other worlds were there that had lost contact with the stars at some point? What did they speak?

Where did he find them?

Sotiria nodded guardedly, so Maddox gestured Riley to move ahead. Trinh was covering, while Murphy and the others spread out and turned their backs to watch for more hungry kitties answering that hunting call.

Maddox just hoped that the species was as individual as house cats. A pack of wolves would be a mess right now. And a lot of destroyed trees because Trinh had her cannon with her.

And ready.

Maddox switched the comm to his left hand, just in case he needed to draw and fire, but the two women seemed calm enough. Riley spoke quietly. The Professor kept up a steady stream of color commentary from the tone, but Maddox didn't follow any of it except when he translated things Stavroula told him.

Still, Sotiria stepped back and let Riley kneel to work. Maddox stayed on his feet, across from Sotiria and watching both for sudden movements.

Stavroula had put her spear down. Wood, with a metal tip that looked sharp. Knife on her waist and a second in her boot, so this was a dangerous world. Sotiria was equally armed but leaning on her spear now instead of threatening anyone.

Good enough.

Face said seventeen, if she was anything like Noelle had been at that age. Young, but presumably an adult in this world. Especially if the two women had slipped out of the woods and visited the dig last night.

Riley got a walking boot out of her pack and wrapped it around Stavroula's ankle, inflating it with a hiss.

"Professor, I've got a Dermal Injector that I can use to numb up her leg," Riley said. "Can you translate that, please?"

More words, followed by a sharp conversation between the two women, Stavroula being stubborn and Sotiria basically telling her to shut up and let the doctor work.

Some things spanned vocabulary.

"Medic Erson, they have some concerns about Stavroula being able to walk if you proceed," the Professor said.

"Professor, ask her how far it is to her village," Maddox suddenly interjected. "If it is close, we can help her limp there or carry her. Or break out the stretcher. Alternatively, *Crime Lab* might be able to land in this clearing since we've got an expert pilot."

More conversation. Sotiria's eyes locked hard on Maddox and scowled, but relented to something.

Then she nodded and said something else.

"Nevin, Sotiria will accept your assistance in getting to their village," the Professor said. "I think it is roughly two kilometers, but they use a different measuring system than I am used to."

He nodded and watched Riley pull out her Dermal Injector and pull Stavroula's leather pant leg up to expose flesh. The device hissed and both women jumped, but almost immediately Stavroula relaxed with a sigh of relief.

Riley looked up.

"She should be mobile," the woman said. "However, that leg is going to be a stump for now. She twisted her ankle pretty badly. Don't think she tore anything, but I also didn't drag out my Quadiprobe to ultrasound the bones. Orders?"

Maddox nodded and handed Riley the comm, moving around until he was on the other side of the young woman. Sotiria backed up, nervous but calm.

Maddox held out his arms and mimicked picking Stavroula up to carry her. She drew a tense breath, then nodded.

He got under her and lifted. Tiny, so she weighed next to nothing. One of her arms went around his neck and he concentrated on not banging her feet as he stood and looked at Sotiria.

"You ready?" he asked. The Professor translated.

Sotiria picked up the other spear and nodded, setting out at a walk.

"Forward team, fall in," Maddox called. "Hoàng, watch for cats on the scanner."

"That's for damned sure," Trinh replied.

The sailors laughed, so the two women relaxed a bit more.

Hopefully, he could get them home safely.

38

Padraig had made small talk with Commander Huffmann on the flight down. Nothing important. Mostly background about the dig, leaving out some of the details she didn't know, but reinforcing that it was a civilian mission to an unknown—and presumably uninhabited and unclaimed world in the middle of nowhere—where they hoped to find planet-bound derelicts that were interesting.

Plus, whatever Maddox Nevin had gotten up to. Padraig wouldn't know until they were on the ground.

Sabahattin was lovely as they descended, angling in from the west and the setting sun to where he could see what Kaitlin and Professor Whitlaw had accomplished. Truly impressive, because the late afternoon sun glinted merrily off of something in the dig.

Hull metal? If so, the mission was already a success.

"Landing now, sir," Rafferty called. "All hands stand by."

Roadrunner landed like a feather under his touch and the rear ramp opened to let in the first smells of trees and nearby ocean.

Padraig was first out, escorting Commander Huffmann and her people down and over to where Kaitlin and Whitlaw were standing. Maddox wasn't in sight, but that didn't mean anything. Cameron Farrell presumably had the dig site secured, because Yua

Kaneko was standing close, covered in dirt and smiling like she'd won a prize.

"Commander Huffmann of the *Traisan* navy, this is my Stevedore, Kaitlin Lynch, and the civilian in charge of the dig, Professor Nicodemus Whitlaw," he said.

Handshakes. Small talk. Walking in the toward the dig, trailing after Kaneko.

"News?" Padraig asked in an open-ended manner.

"We have located and partially excavated what appears to be an early *Riffrost*-era cargo vessel," the Professor replied. "We were about to open it when news of visitors arrived, so we took the afternoon largely off and presumed that they would like to be present for such a momentous occasion."

"Early *Riffrost* era?" Huffmannasked, stepping a little closer to probe.

"So I believe, based on subtle cues," Whitlaw replied. "Are you familiar with the period?"

"Academically," Huffmann said. "The *Traisan Monarchy* was one of the first groups to splinter out of *Riffrost*, before we absorbed the Reedy Commonwealth."

Padraig liked the way she finessed that particular war of conquest. *Absorbed.* Almost sounded friendly.

"After *Naara* disintegrated, *Riffrost* represented a variety of technological innovations, as well as aesthetic ones," Whitlaw nodded, shifting into lecture mode as the group walked. "Those cues led me to certain expectations, but we cannot know for sure until we board, which I'm hoping will happen shortly. Gary, are you ready?"

"That oil should have had all afternoon to work into the machinery, Professor," Renshaw replied from a corner.

"There you have it," Whitlaw beamed. "Shortly."

They crossed the gap quickly and it became obvious that a tremendous amount of work had been completed, exposing one corner of a hillside to show the ship or object underneath.

"Gary, would you do the honors?" Whitlaw asked as the group gathered around the obvious hatch.

The skinny man got flat and torqued hard on a wheel that looked just like how *A'Zedi* ships did their manual overrides for airlocks. After a few moments, the hatch itself popped audibly and hissed.

"That is dead air inside off-gassing and mixing with healthy atmosphere," Whitlaw announced.

"Dead?" Huffmann queried.

"We presume it was buried and sealed," the Professor answered. "Anything like bacteria or the like that needed oxygen would eventually consume it all, leaving only nitrogen or carbon dioxide. We'll need to let the hatch remain open for a few minutes, then hopefully we can penetrate the interior, as long as we're careful."

"Sir, we've got air masks," Farrell called. "Same thing happens in space, so I grabbed a box from the fire-fighting gear just in case."

Padraig laughed at the look of honest shock on Whitlaw's face. And the rest of the civilians.

"Break them out, Farrell," Padraig called.

Kaneko grabbed a crate and pulled open the top, handing out several.

He smiled as folks started pulling on masks and babbling excitedly.

"Professor, you should lead us," Padraig offered. "Renshaw as well, since you've been so deeply involved. Commander Huffmann and Lieutenant Schmidt, let us see what the past left for us."

39

———

Nicodemus wanted to cry. There was simply no emotion left at the peak of his existence save an overwhelming burst of excitement at having come so far and seen so much.

Kaitlin Lynch had specifically ordered everyone not to mention what Maddox Nevin had discovered. Or how Nicodemus had helped apparently rescue a pair of teenage girl cousins, who were even now being transported to their village by Nevin and his team.

Presumably, that would be the other shoe that got dropped on the strangers in a while. Possibly over dinner.

Nicodemus had a handlamp. And his Monitoring Datalog, turned on and sampling everything it could record as he stepped to the threshold and steeled himself to enter.

Pride, that was what it was. He'd been doubted. Belittled. Ostracized. Exiled.

And he had been *right*, all along.

Plus, nobody on the mission save him could have talked to the locals, however poorly he felt he'd done so. At least he'd been there.

Darkness, cut by the lamp. Cargo space from the way it

169

stretched all the way across some eighteen meters and possibly up three decks of hollow volume inside.

And Oh! My! Gods! there were a few crates in here. Boxes, hopefully containing something historic. Valuable. Academic. Something.

Nicodemus stepped onto the ancient deck and shined his light around. Cargo bay indeed, with the outlines of broadside cargo bay doors on both sides when he looked. Engine room to his right. Corridors forward, currently empty, so whoever had left the ship here hadn't locked it all down and forced whoever came next to go through it opening hatch by hatch.

"Entering the cargo bay," he said for the audio recorder on his Datalog. "Possible cargo in crates to inspect later, but I am turning forward to see what there might be. The ship does not appear to have been emptied before abandonment, but I cannot determine its state at present."

"They were in kinda a hurry," Ms. Kaneko said from his hip, causing him to turn and look at the woman. "Bay stuff would have been pushed off the side to be emptied on the soil. But they simply said fuck it, closed everything up, and left. Those boxes should have been strapped down for flight."

Oh, that made sense. Cargo had mostly been emptied, but then something had caused the crew to leave? War? Disaster? Plague?

"Moving forward up the portside corridor," he continued narrating as he led his small troupe of explorers. "Hallway is open and contains only the dirt we are tracking in at present. We'll need to sweep it all back out later, but that can wait. There appear to be no power sources visible on my various scans. I see multiple side hatchways to explore later, but I am moving all the way forward now to locate the bridge. Somewhere, there will be stairs or ladders up to what should be two other decks."

"Professor," Captain Boru interrupted. "Would datacores have survived this long, or are we beyond even long-term semi-volatile states?"

"Presumably, the cores would have simply lost internal power," Nicodemus replied. "If they are shielded sufficiently, they might still be readable. My hope is to be able to extract them and attempt such a task."

"I'll have you work with my Radio Officer," Boru said. "She's exceptional at that sort of thing. It's come up a few times on previous missions."

"Good to know, Captain," Nicodemus nodded, somewhat relieved because he'd been expecting to have to apply for a whole other grant to cover the sorts of experts and tools to reconstruct ancient computer cores.

The corridor was wide enough for two people to easily walk abreast, so Nicodemus presumed carts of a standard size. The hatches ran almost the full width and height, flat to the deck, so that reinforced his impressions.

Forward, following his light and keeping up a running commentary that he could review later when he compared sensor settings and decided where to look closer.

The odds were that the ship could not be dug out and flown away. At least not without a tremendous amount of time, effort, and cash that he simply didn't have. Hopefully, someone could land a large transport and lift the whole thing, though Nicodemus wasn't certain that such an act would be entirely legal.

Not if there were humans who lived here, however primitive.

Legal precedence versus salvage rights. Maybe he could convince them to turn it into an in-place museum? There were several other hills here to be explored, and this already justified a second mission, even if Nicodemus couldn't convince Captain Boru to have someone send out a resupply vessel at some point.

What could he find?

"Approaching the bridge now, I believe," he said. "At least that is my translation of the sign. Taking a picture for confirmation and translation later."

He was pretty certain, though. Talking to the young woman

native had brought a lot of old language lessons to the fore in his mind.

Discovery.

And the hatchway was open. He took a deep breath in spite of his mask and stepped into the original command space. Two stations where folks would sit while flying, both facing a long console with spaces beside them that both could control. More stations around the sides of the room, plus a couple of hatches that should lead to storage, a toilet, and maybe a break room or an astro-telemetry space with old maps, because many people kept binders as a backup to losing their nav computer data, even today.

"Command space," he said, moving to the station on the left, where *Riffrost* traditionally set their pilot, with a copilot to the right handling secondary tasks like engines, power, life support, or whatever.

Ahead of him, the window coverings were open, showing dirt packed on the transsteel windows.

"Blast shields are open, so we can measure off the correct distance and clear them," he spoke aloud."

"Ninety-three meters from the hatch," Kaneko offered, so he knew where she was digging next.

They shared a conspiratorial grin. He'd have had to look at his sensor readings to be that accurate. She'd apparently paced it. They made a good team.

Nicodemus turned to Captain Boru and Commander Huffmann.

"We have, as near as I can tell, discovered a lost and abandoned *Riffrost* cargo transport, with some cargo still aboard plus whatever secondary gear and personal effects may have been left behind when the ship was abandoned," he stated formally. "As such, I am placing a claim on the dig, an area of roughly eighty to one hundred hectares that includes this vessel and several other potential spots nearby that might be other ships or ground facilities, which have yet to be determined. Roughly the area where we have tentatively identified a buried tarmac indicating the original flight line."

There. Formal. Official.

LEGAL.

At least as legal as he could get, until they knew what Maddox had found.

And how the natives would react.

Nicodemus noted how Captain Boru turned to the two strangers, inviting them to speak without offering an opinion first. But then, they'd all gone over the treaties that would cover this, both before and after confirming human habitation.

That other shoe.

"What are your intentions with the dig?" the woman asked pertly.

"Find out who lived here," Nicodemus replied. "The vessels were last seen four centuries or so ago, before they were buried. This was some sort of starport, but we're only just beginning to uncover anything useful. The ships and whatever buildings we find might have technological value, as will the potential cargo, but we cannot determine that until we do a more in-depth study. Will the *Enlightened Tyranny* be planning to claim this world? It currently lies outside your recognized borders, but yours is the closest major power by galactic distance."

He left it at that. Boru nodded subtly, pretty much forcing the strangers to have an opinion.

Nicodemus didn't know what was happening in orbit, but things seemed calm, and *Marrakesh*'s crew had struck him with their professional demeanor.

The woman turned to study Captain Boru, largely ignoring the rest of them, but Nicodemus wasn't offended. This had just become a matter between star nations.

And Boru still had a trump card in his back pocket.

40

Padraig watched Huffmann ponder her options. Schmidt surprised her and everyone else by taking a step forward to address the Professor.

"Are there other archaeological sites on this planet?" he asked simply.

Padraig watched the Professor turn toward, as if asking for help.

"We have been conducting a formal survey from orbit," Padraig explained. "As yet, we have located no radio signals or other technological indicators. It will take much longer to determine where other ruins might have been covered over time. We knew where to begin here because Professor Whitlaw had planetary coordinates and descriptions we were able to match. A full survey will take more time, but I will remind everyone that this is a civilian operation chartered under an *A'Zedi* government exoarchaeological research grant."

He left it at that, mostly to see how much leeway he might have with the two of them. Or how much they might have from their captain. And superiors back home.

"What do you expect to find?" Huffmann asked, looking back and forth between him and the Professor.

"Perhaps a couple of other ships buried here from what I've been told," Padraig spoke first. "Ground facilities like hangars or control spaces for a small starport. Given the state of this vessel, I expect that they might even be intact. Professor, what would you say is the state of technology here, just from what you can see on this bridge?"

Whitlaw paused and turned slowly in place. Others did the same.

"Early *Riffrost* suggests significantly more primitive technology than we have today," the Professor said. "Much slower Ghostdrives, probably only capable of a burst speeds up to Mark Four, as a historical rule. And even that was an improvement over *Naara* vessels, which often could not exceed Mark One, and instead usually measured their speeds in light-years per day."

"Armaments?" Padraig asked, pushing the conversation over into places that could be reported to Captain Gerhardt in orbit.

"A cargo ship like this might not have any, Captain Boru," the Professor replied. "I can't be certain what other ships might lay buried until we do some exploratory digging and perhaps scan the hills closer to differentiate ships from buildings. At least three have the appearance of being collapsed buildings or hangars. Possibly five, though those might have collapsed onto something parked inside. Again, we cannot know at present."

Padraig turned to Huffmann and silently asked her opinion.

"How soon will you know?" she asked.

"Our mission allotted seventy-five days in the field," Padraig told her. "With the notion that an important enough find might rate having another transport haul out supplies to let us stay on station longer."

"But not to build a permanent base?" she pressed.

"I will remind you again that this is a civilian-led exoarchaeology mission," he said. "I don't make policy, so I cannot speak for my superiors, but they could have sent along a pod that could be deployed into a small orbital facility, had they chosen. And they still might, but I cannot know until I file my first report and hear back from them. However, I've seen what I need from the interior, Professor, so we'll need to transmit data, pictures, and reports. I presume that Commander Huffmann's superiors might wish to view a copy of that report?"

He turned to her for confirmation and got it.

"Then we should retire to the main camp for now, given how late in the day it is," Padraig continued. "Professor Whitlaw and his folks can continue their work tomorrow, both identifying this vessel as best they can and surveying the rest of the site for which spots might prove the most fruitful for the next stage of things."

He waited for the two strangers to nod, then started walking, leaving Whitlaw and Kaneko behind as he led the other dozen folks out into the fading sunlight.

Dinner time would fall shortly. And he still had Nevin's secondary mission to deal with, which felt like why Chance had asked—practically ordered—him to come to the surface.

The groups split in two, with him leading Huffmann and her people. Kaitlin had largely remained silent through all this, but she smiled at him now as they smelled dinner cooking.

Then his comm chirped.

"Boru," he said, opening it.

"Nevin, sir," Maddox replied. "I've spoken with Squire Taggart and she tells me you are on the surface with *Traisan* visitors?"

"That's correct, Armiger," Padraig said. "What's your situation?"

"Positive, Captain," Maddox replied. "But a bit complicated."

41

Maddox had done pretty well carrying Stavroula while following Sotiria back down the slope a little and around. He smelled the village long before he saw it, with wood smoke drifting through the trees.

Sotiria led them to a small stream, then started uphill following the bank. She kept up a quiet, running commentary, pointing at various things and speaking single words, so Maddox assumed that she was teaching him her language and repeated them. A few times, she even smiled, however tightly it looked.

Stavroula had kind of settled in his arms, leaning into him and possibly dozing, but that might be the medication, because the trail wasn't all that smooth. Still, they got there.

Wherever there was.

A wall, made of vertical tree trunks lashed and maybe glued together, generally ten meters tall with a couple of what his mind wanted to call fighting platforms. People on the platforms watching, holding primitive crossbows.

Sotiria called something and the folks up there seemed to relax some. An open gate in the wall suddenly appeared when she led them around a corner. Several folks stood in the opening, holding spears or things somewhere between swords and maces by shape.

About half men. Big men. The other half were women ranging from Sotiria's age up to one old crone who might be her great-grandmother and looked more dangerous than any of the guys Maddox could see.

"Field team, exercise caution here," Maddox ordered in a quiet voice that didn't suggest to the newcomers how close Trinh might be to unleashing havoc if provoked.

Sotiria called something as well and the guards at the gate relaxed. One of the women stepped forward, looking like an authority figure. Maybe Captain Boru's age. Maybe had kids Sotiria's age.

Armed with a spear. And a hard scowl. Maddox didn't want to drop Stavroula, and wasn't sure she could even hobble, but if trouble broke out, he'd be in a world of hurt.

At least until his team escalated things way out beyond ugly.

"She didn't break her leg," Maddox said simply as the woman stepped close. "Twisted it badly and we've immobilized it and given her something for the pain and swelling."

Woman didn't understand a word he said, but Stavroula perked up and spoke. Sotiria, too. Long conversation in whatever dialect it was. Maddox recognized about one word in ten, not counting the names of the two girls.

The native security team wasn't too bad when it came to tactics and organization. They stayed arrayed in a sort of half circle, plus a few folks up on the wall watching, those folks armed with bows.

Idly, he wondered if Trinh would annihilate the wall first. She could. None of them were really organized for combat operations today. And he didn't think they should be, because this was some sort of First Contact.

Woman in charge stepped closer. Fortyish. Mom, honestly, from the way she looked at the two girls, though he wasn't sure whose.

"Maddox?" she said, causing him to jump in surprise.

He nodded.

"Chrysa," the woman said, touching her chest.

"Nice to meet you, Chrysa," he said automatically.

Sotiria stepped close and tugged on his arm, still speaking a running commentary and gesturing for him to go with her and Chrysa into the village.

Inside the walls.

At least those walls wouldn't hold up long if he had to get out later.

"Okay," he said. "Riley, you're with me. Hoàng, you take Murphy and the rest and back off to provide a rescue team if we need it. If you do not hear from me in an hour, call on the comm and expect me to say *goldbug* as a password. Anything else, you've got trouble and call the Captain."

"Understood, sir," Trinh replied. "But I'm calling Cam first."

"Deal."

He nodded to the two women and started walking. The others in the greeting party watched his group split and were concerned, but Chrysa said something and they moved inside, however grumbly they might be.

Not that I don't trust you folks, but we've only just met and I don't speak Riffrost.

He smiled. Carried Stavroula carefully.

The inside of the compound had been pounded flat by a lot of feet, but there were still trees inside so Nyssa might not have seen this place from orbit unless she knew where to look. Or scanned for his comm signature, which she probably was doing, come to think of it. She was a lot smarter than he was. Than most of them were. She'd keep his ass safe.

Chrysa led, apparently ordering the others to go back to what they were doing, until it was only her and that dangerous old woman as they approached a long, low building made of planks slathered over with some kind of mud, maybe as insulation?

Maddox didn't know. Couldn't ask. Could pay attention and learn.

Chrysa entered first. The old woman went next. Sotiria led

and made sure he followed, with Riley close on his heels and nobody else.

Interior was a wood floor, polished smooth and covered over with pretty, woven rugs. Stone fireplace burning on one side. Art on wood walls. Nice furniture, all of it wood as well, but covered in wool cloth knitted like a sweater he occasionally wore off-duty.

Most of the folks he'd seen were wearing leather from animals, which was still just weird. And a few wool things. Or maybe a kind of cotton.

Obviously, he needed to do more homework on primitive societies.

Sotiria led him to a kind of couch and gestured, so he gently set Stavroula down. She had a smile for him that he returned.

Weird day, but it had turned out well so far.

Chrysa started to talk, but the old woman interrupted.

"Galini," she introduced herself, also touching her chest.

"Maddox," he said, then pointed to his medic. "Riley."

She repeated the words, then strung a whole bunch on the back, mostly questions.

He shrugged. Sotiria and Stavroula started a long explanation. Lots of back and forth.

At one point, Maddox realized that he was the only male in the room, which was just odd, but a point he filed.

Matriarchal society? They weren't that common in the wider galaxy, with *A'Zedi* being pretty equal that way, same as *Wronlori*. *Traisa* was a little male-dominated and the *Holy Imperium of Copez* largely considered women as secondary citizens.

Finally, Sotiria turned to him and pointed at the pocket where his comm was, making a hand gesture like holding the device when the Professor had been talking.

He checked the time and called Trinh first.

"Hoàng."

"Nevin," he said. "First check in is good. *Goldbug* here. Reset one hour on your timer."

"Understood, sir."

He nodded and swapped to a different number.

"*Marrakesh*, Taggart."

"Nyssa, it's Maddox," he said. "I'm in the native village, having returned the girls and met what might be the chief and a village elder, both female. This feels kinda big. Is the Captain available? I'm right at the edge of what standing orders and even galactic treaties cover, as far as I can tell."

"Captain's planetside, Armiger," she replied in a formal tone. "Commander Messier has the deck, but you should probably contact him directly. The visitor is a small *Traisan* patrol craft, and they sent some observers down to the dig. Captain escorted them and they've been on the ground for about an hour. I do not believe they've been told about your mission yet."

Maddox paused and digested that.

First Contact, and the *Enlightened Tyranny* would be present, too. Kinda extra-messy at that point, but also useful because that was two sets of governments involved.

"Understood, Radio," he said. "Out."

He looked up at Sotiria and shrugged again, as if to say, hang on a moment while I try something else.

The two older women had both jumped at the talking box in his hand, but neither of the younger ones had, so everyone was calm.

Maddox drew a deep breath and dialed the Captain's number.

"Boru," the Captain was there instantly.

"Nevin, sir," Maddox replied. "I've spoken with Squire Taggart and she tells me you are on the surface with *Traisan* visitors?"

"That's correct, Armiger," the Captain asked sharply. "What's your situation?"

"Positive, Captain," Maddox told him. "But a bit complicated."

"How so?"

"Is the Professor handy?" Maddox asked. "I need his linguistic abilities."

"Why is that, Armiger?" Captain pressed.

Maddox considered his words carefully, then decided that maybe the Captain wanted this blown up big.

"Because I've made First Contact with the native population, sir," Maddox said, damning all consequences. "They are human as far as I can tell but living a primitive lifestyle at an Iron Age technology level. Professor Whitlaw understands their dialect and I am currently speaking with a village chief and an elder. Or will be shortly."

He blew out a heavy breath and waited, wondering just how much trouble he was going to be in for this. Captain Boru might just break him for his actions, even if everything had looked proper at the time.

"Maddox, it's Nicodemus." The Professor was suddenly on the line. "I take it you got Stavroula and Sotiria home safely?"

"Affirmative, sir," Maddox said.

Both of the younger women had perked up to hear the Professor speak. He addressed them now and the older ladies jumped.

Maddox fell entirely out of the conversation at that point, other than to hold the comm as others spoke around him.

He almost felt like a kid at some adult party, standing around largely invisible, save that Chrysa reached out a hand at one point and squeezed his arm gently. Nothing more, but it conveyed volumes and he finally found a way to relax a bit.

The old woman's smile lifted the rest of the weight off his shoulders. Some of those men had been big, but she'd been the only one who'd really scared him. Not a woman to mess with.

Finally, the conversation wound down.

"Maddox, it's Captain Boru," and he perked right back up.

The Professor said something in their tongue and all four women were all eyes, too.

"Go ahead, sir," Maddox replied.

"It is late in the day and Taggart has you triangulated roughly fifteen kilometers north-north-west of the dig," the Captain continued. "Professor Whitlaw thinks that landing a shuttle close by would frighten folks. The Chief there, Chrysa, has invited your party to stay with them tonight under some pretty interesting guest traveler customs, so Whitlaw thinks you will be safe. Tomorrow, I want you reporting back to the dig on foot. Be careful, but I don't think you are at any risk from the natives. They claim to owe you a life debt for rescuing the girls."

"Understood, sir," Maddox replied. "We'll be off as soon as it is light enough to hike safely."

"See you then, Sailor," the Captain said. "And good job, Maddox. Boru out."

Maddox blew out a sigh that felt like most of his innards wanted to escape with it.

Honest-to-freaking-gods. First Contact. Him. And he hadn't screwed it up.

Yet, he amended.

He nodded to the women and let himself relax a little more.

42

Padraig had been watching Commander Huffmann and especially Lieutenant Schmidt as the conversation progressed. The younger man had nearly lost his shit when the scope of things changed so radically.

This was suddenly an inhabited world. With a native population that was currently in contact with the *A'Zedi* government. It might be a civilian dig, but Padraig was the Fleet in situations like this.

With all the legal ramifications therein.

"See you then, Sailor," Padraig smiled. "And good job, Maddox. Boru out."

He closed his comm and slid it into a pocket, smiling ever-so-slightly at the two across from him.

"Thank you, Professor," he said, giving Huffmann time to find her breath. "It sounds like you and Armiger Nevin handled that situation excellently."

"Maddox did all the hard work, Captain," the Professor replied. "I simply provided translation services when he rescued a pair of young ladies that had been chased by a large cat-like creature, leaving one of them injured. His team deserves all the credit for that, and I frankly find myself looking forward to meeting them at some point. Obviously, we're probably trespassing to some extent, but I'm hoping that some of Maddox's goodwill rubs off here and they allow us to continue our work. Possibly even help in whatever manner they might."

"What happens to your situation, Professor Whitlaw, as this world is inhabited?" Commander Huffmann asked finally.

Padraig watched the man shrug eloquently.

"There are any number of treaties that cover this sort of thing, madam," he replied evenly. "I will presume that the people Armiger Nevin met represent some manner of planetary government until I'm convinced otherwise. As such, I will attempt to negotiate whatever commercial or academic agreement I can that allows me to continue my dig, possibly extracting valuable goods that can be sold to various museums in such a way that the effort further finances my archaeology while also benefiting the natives. It sounds like they are primitives to some extent, so exposure to the wider galaxy will have both benefits and problems that will need to be addressed. I cannot know how they got here until such time as we have a deeper conversation and learn their history better. Assuming, of course, that they know themselves. I presume they are the descendants of a planetary population that chose to remain when the others left, or were somehow lost sailors unable to be rescued and making the best of what they had. In that case, falling to an Iron Age civilization is a relatively quick thing, and stable over a long-enough term, given that the availability of refined metals should be high."

He paused there and watched the newcomers. Padraig smiled when Commander Huffmann turned to look at him, then he interrupted her before she could say anything.

"Commander, I think it might be beneficial if Captain Gerhardt joined us in the morning," he offered. "That puts *Traisa* on an equal footing with *A'Zedi*, as we'll both be represented by commanding officers when we formally meet the locals."

He left it at that. Schmidt nodded so compactly that Padraig almost missed it, but that man understood how big this might have just gotten, over and above the possible value of old ships.

Not necessarily a technological revolution waiting to be found, but a social and political one, since Sabahattin was inhabited.

How many other worlds in this region might have similar stories to tell?

Huffmann turned to her assistant and they shared a nod.

"With your permission, we'll withdraw for a bit of privacy, Captain," she said.

He nodded.

"Cam, you go with them in case there are any of those predators running around," Kaitlin ordered sharply. "You will not tell anyone on this crew anything that you overhear as a result, short of a senior flag officer overruling my orders. Am I clear?"

Padraig watched Farrell snap to, then nod.

"Sir, yes, sir," she barked automatically.

"And she will," Kaitlin told them. "I think you'll be safest if you head out that direction, maybe a third of the way to the dig itself where we have sensors on both sides watching."

"Thank you, Stevedore Lynch," she said.

Huffmann and Schmidt took their two unarmed bodyguards, and let Farrell lead them off. Folks watched from a distance, but they could have a private conversation while safe from over-sized cats.

He turned to Whitlaw and Renshaw, drawing them both in, Kaneko, and Kaitlin in closer.

"So what the hell has been going on down here?" he asked with a smile.

Their laughter was good, then folks started walking him through all those little details of their day and Padraig found that he couldn't be prouder of his crew and his civilians.

They had done good, in all the right ways.

43

———

Maddox had slept on a bed filled with branches of a local tree. Evergreen needles of a sort he didn't know, save that they were pretty comfortable, and smelled piney every time he'd rolled over.

Not that he'd slept much, but enough. And there would be more coffee back at the camp to revitalize him later. They'd used up a good chunk of what they'd brought.

The windows were closed with shutters, but enough light crept in to show him the impending dawn, even as the fire in the fireplace had been kept going all night by Sotiria or Galini.

Nobody had bothered his team in here, and his folks had largely rotated a quiet watch, with someone always awake.

Morning.

He rose and got introduced to how you handled human waste on a primitive world, where things were collected for fertilizer and other basic chemical ingredients. And he met a bunch of nosy sheep that wanted to sniff him when he got walked over to their barn.

Weird. But he supposed that this had been how humanity had lived before starflight and galactic civilization, wherever they had come from.

Nobody really knew. Or rather, there were so many

competing stories out there that nobody could say which was the truth.

And most naval folks didn't have time to look when there was another war with *Wronlori* ongoing. Or the latest installment of a war dating back a century.

Chrysa offered breakfast, but Maddox only sampled a few things to be polite, while the crew broke out self-heating meal-packs and offered bites to whoever wanted some.

Pantomime for the most part. Sure, words, but few anybody understood as yet.

Nervous, but not hostile. Careful, so as to not give offense or step over any hidden lines.

Somehow, Maddox wasn't surprised when Chrysa and Galini made it clear that they were accompanying Sotiria as she led them back to the dig. Murphy could have done it probably almost as easily, but this was a political statement.

First Contact.

One of those places in the journey of life where the path you had been on suddenly intersects with a different one, offering you alternatives if you wanted to reach out and grab them.

Crossroads.

A new beginning for the folks of Sabahattin, one way or the other, because now the wider galaxy would know that they were here. And *Traisa* would have to recalibrate things on this frontier, the same as Survey Corps would have to stretch out their maps to encompass a new zone.

There was a gap between *Wronlori* and *Traisa* that you could navigate, if you were careful about those other various crossroads. Going anti-spinward and rimward, there was a big gap between *Traisa* and *Copez*, same as there was if you went straight coreward from *A'Zedi*.

Lots of places Survey Corps might look for folks like this.

What other crossroads were out there?

Stavroula had obviously been pissed about being left behind, but Maddox had missed that conversation save for the emotions going back and forth. Instead they walked south towards the morning sun and downhill, eventually emerging from the trees to see the dig, the camp, and several shuttles on the ground with folks at work.

Farrell was up in her tower keeping watch, because she called almost as soon as they hit grasslands.

"Nevin," he said, drawing out his comm when it chirped.

"That you?" she asked.

"Affirmative," Maddox said. "My team, plus three native representatives to meet the Captain."

"*Traisan* captain came down first thing this morning, sir," she informed him. "They'll all be there to meet you at the main camp. Dig team is shoveling as fast as they can, just in case they get thrown off the planet today."

Why would they...? Oh, right.

"Understood, Farrell," he replied. "See you shortly."

He pocketed the device and smiled at the ladies when they silently asked what was going on.

"Going home," he told them with a nod, keeping pace.

That was another crossroads down there in the distance, waiting for him.

44

Padraig had risen early. Breakfasted with the digging crew hurrying to get as much done as they could today, scanning every one of the other mounds for anything that would identify at least which to save for last if nothing else.

He and Kaitlin then had coffee with Captain Gerhardt and his people. Padraig was a little sad that Chance had to remain on the ship, but somebody had to be in charge up there, even with Gerhardt down on the planet and little risk that *Baldur Schreiber* might do anything stupid.

An utterly momentous day.

His comm chirped.

"Boru," he said.

"Taggart, sir," Nyssa replied. "Signals place our team just inside the edge of the forest and headed your way now. ETA about forty-five minutes at their current pace."

"Understood, Radio," he said. "When you have a chance later, Professor Whitlaw will be digging in the wreck for their datacores. I'd like you to assist him in data-recovery operations."

"Stevedore Lynch updated me last night, sir," Nyssa replied. "I've got a variety of things on tap as soon as he's ready. About half are portable enough to transport to the surface if necessary."

"You take charge of determining that, Taggart," he ordered. "And handle it."

One less thing on his plate, in a day with a lot of delicate diplomacy to handle.

"Aye, sir."

"Boru out." He smiled at the others.

"Any last thoughts before we make history?" he asked Captain Gerhardt.

"You are taking this with remarkable aplomb, Captain Boru," the man replied.

"I've got a good crew," he told the man, leaving off nearly everything important. "They can handle things. Sabahattin is far from our borders, so not a place likely to deal directly with *A'Zedi* that much, save when we come specifically to talk to them or dig up old salvage. And everyone has signed all the treaties covering these situations. Whitlaw might be over-emphasizing the local governance issues, but he wants to get formal permission to keep digging because he has folks in *Wronlori* that he wants to show up with his discoveries."

"You don't consider these people a planetary government?" Schmidt spoke up with the sorts of hungry linguistic precision you got from lawyers.

"On the contrary, I do," Padraig corrected the man. "They are not, however, likely prepared to handle interstellar politics and diplomacy on this scale if they only woke up yesterday and realized that they were the children of star travelers. Part of my job will be to help educate them on their rights and responsibilities as an inhabited and currently *Unaligned* planet, acting as something of an ambassador, both for them and to them. It is my hope that *A'Zedi* will send out someone formally, just as I am certain that you have asked the Supreme Autocrat to do the same."

Gerhardt nodded at that, but Padraig wasn't surprised. Being captain of a vessel was more than just being the commanding officer on the deck. You had a vast array of responsibilities that tended to be wide open because communications back to head-quarters might take days at this kind of distance.

"And if they tell you to depart immediately?" Huffmann asked, possibly assigned the role of the heavy here.

"Then we pack up and go," Padraig nodded. "I would presume that you would do the same. It would be in poor taste if someone decided to invade and occupy this world, especially if they are at such a technological disadvantage."

He left the threat vague. *A'Zedi* might not do anything if *Traisa* did, but they might. Better if everyone exercised care instead.

The others left it alone and the conversation turned to less important matters. Climate. Wild speculation about how Sabahattin had come to be inhabited originally, as well as what had happened subsequently.

Eventually, he saw figures drawing close. From the dig, Professor Whitlaw emerged and started toward the camp, leaving most of the team behind, apparently under the joint command of Gary Renshaw and Expert Sailor Kaneko from the looks of it.

Dangerous pair of conspirators.

Padraig rose and led his group over to where the gate in the wire fence was open for the day. Maddox Nevin's team were obvious, escorting three women. Padraig had to smile that their ages matched the old mythos of *Maid, Mother, and Crone*, but he wasn't sure how many people around him would get that reference.

"Field Team, returning from a successful mission," Maddox said in a proud, tired voice as he came to rest.

Professor Whitlaw seemed happy to simply translate, standing off to one side and quickly repeating things. Padraig made sure to speak slowly and clearly to help.

"More than merely successful, Armiger Nevin," Padraig assured him. "This is one of those gold star moments that will follow you for the rest of your career. Possibly the rest of your life."

Padraig liked the impact those words had on the young man, his chest puffing up a little and shoulders going back. Eyes glittering with some bright emotions.

"Sir, thank you," Maddox said. "This is Sotiria, who we rescued yesterday along with her kinswoman Stavroula who was unable to make the walk. Chrysa, who is the village chief where we stayed last night. Galini, who is a respected elder."

Padraig agreed on the respected part. Both women deferred unconsciously to her in stance. And the woman had a proud smile on her face as she heard the Professor speak.

"I am Captain Padraig Boru, of *A'Zedi*," he introduced himself. "Captain Dennis Gerhardt of *Traisa*. We are both visitors to your world from a great distance away."

He waited as that got conveyed, then went on and introduced Kaitlin and the Professor, as well as Huffmann and Schmidt. History being made, however slowly.

"Captain, Chrysa asks if you command everyone, or represent two groups here," Whitlaw said at one point.

"Tell her three, including yourself as civilian archaeologists, Professor," Padraig replied. Then he turned to the Stevedore. "Kaitlin, this is your camp. I'll let you take charge of this."

And she was a woman, roughly midway in age between the older two, in what appeared to be a matriarchal society.

Quickly, everyone got moved to a central spot in the wardroom tent. Tea and coffee were served and explained, along with some fresh pastries that had been baked special for this morning. Bland but sweet.

Breaking bread, as it were, with all the historical, cultural, and social implications that came with it.

Whitlaw never stopped speaking, but hardly addressed anyone, instead translating everything on the fly and doing a pretty good job of it.

"Sky ship?" Sotiria asked point blank at one point, causing everyone to goggle, even though she was staring directly at him.

"Correct," Padraig nodded. "Starship."

That got through, so she was picking up words along the way quickly.

"She asks what the galaxy is like," Whitlaw expanded. "Well, she used a term that was something like sky plateau, but that's the implication I got."

"Maddox, draw her a rough map," Padraig ordered, putting his new survey expert on the spot.

Paper was found and scribed. *A'Zedi* in the middle. *Wronlori* Spinward across a wide arc. *Traisa* to Rimward. *Copez* Anti-Spinward and Coreward some. Lots of blank space yet to be filled in, dating back to both *Riffrost* and *Naara*.

And points earlier, currently unknown.

The women gasped when the term *light-year* was explained. Then gasped again when the math became clear behind the distance to Horwin. Even sailing so many days was astonishing, but they deserved to know. And it was his responsibility as captain of the vessel making first contact to educate them.

Their entire civilization had just changed. He had to make it for the better.

"Galini asks us to confirm that the cargo ship cannot fly," the Professor asked at one point. "I have explained how old and presumably broken it is. All three women have expressed an interest in visiting space to see *Marrakesh*, but I have not made any promises."

Padraig turned to Gerhardt.

"Unless you have an objection, Captain?" he asked.

"I do not, Captain Boru," the man answered. "As noted, there will be diplomats sent this direction soon enough. It would help if the locals understood better what was out there."

He turned back to the women and nodded.

"Maddox, you take charge of that," he ordered.

"Stavroula might also be interested in that, sir," Maddox replied. "She was disappointed at not being here today."

"As you see fit, Armiger," Padraig smiled. "Kaitlin, you let me know what you need. Professor, are they evicting you from your dig?"

"They are not," Whitlaw grinned. "They are quite interested in what can be found, but understand it to be more in the nature of trade goods that can bring in technology and merchants later, rather than their own ship they can fly."

"Do they remember their past?" he pressed.

"I have been asking and listening, Captain Boru," Whitlaw said. "They have legends of coming from the sky but thought those to be only fanciful myths of ancient gods, as no significant records have survived down to the present. Obviously, that will change. Oh, and Galini tells of first explorers, at least those were her words, and a war among the gods casting all humans down."

"Late *Naara* to early *Riffrost* might qualify," Padraig nodded. "And the ship dates to that era."

"How much do we tell them about the galaxy?" Whitlaw asked.

"As much as they want to know," Padraig replied.

It was their world. He was just visiting.

45

———————

Padraig was sitting on his accustomed bench in the waiting lounge of the *A'Zedi* Intelligence Services main Bureau. Wearing his good uniform, not the one he wore to formal celebrations where all the medals were necessary. Nyssa Taggart sat serenely on his right, no doubt thinking devious thoughts about all the information she had managed to extract from Nicodemus Whitlaw's ancient data-cores, back on Sabahattin.

Fleet had sent out a replacement vessel for *Marrakesh*, rather than sending cargo resupply, so he'd left Whitlaw and the others while returning to base. Diplomats and some trade gear intended to start bringing Sabahattin up to a more modern standard, swapping for the presumed value of the archaeological dig. *Traisa* had started doing something similar, but had not been able to move as quickly.

It helped, being under direct orders of *A'Zedi* Intelligence, where the First Secretary could make things happen immediately when she wanted to.

It was the figure on Padraig's left that put a smile on his face. Maddox Nevin was extremely nervous to be here. Doubly so because he understood what this room, this building, really represented.

Still, the young man had brought honor and glory on himself and his shipmates with his work. And had, according to Nyssa and Kaitlin quietly reporting things, reached his own personal crossroads, which seemed to be the word everyone had used to describe the mission to Sabahattin.

A door opened behind the two older bureaucrats on the other side of the counter and First Secretary Gelashvili stood there, smiling and resplendent.

"Captain. Squire. Armiger," she said grandly. "Would you join me, please?"

Padraig appreciated that she always asked politely, even when she could simply order him to do just about anything. The group of them rose and made their way back, but the First Secretary was using one of the other rooms today, instead of the office Padraig knew.

It turned out to be a conference room. Small, but larger than her space, with a polished wood oval table and six chairs.

"There's coffee and tea," she gestured as she moved to the far side of the table and sat behind a steaming mug.

Padraig went and got himself some, letting that moment bleed some of the tension out of the other two as they waited, then did the same.

Finally, everyone settled.

"Excellent work, Captain," she began. "As always. Squire Taggart, Survey Corps has put you in for an award for being able to recover so much of Whitlaw's data and subsequently translate it into modern coordinates that they can use to search for previously-unknown worlds."

Padraig didn't think a woman as dark-skinned as Nyssa Taggart could darken as she blushed, but she did. Her shaved skull almost turned black.

"Thank you, sir," she stammered. "Mostly, putting other tools to a better use than merely cracking enemy codes."

"Understood, Squire," Gelashvili nodded. "However, some of my technical experts expressed surprise at what you could do, so they wish to take you aside at some point and pick your brain. Possibly have you teach a few classes here to pass along your knowledge."

And she blushed even darker this time, to the point Padraig wondered if she might pass out. But she did start breathing again quickly enough.

He smiled at her.

"And Armiger Nevin." The First Secretary turned to the newest member of this little conspiracy. "Welcome, and exceptional work yourself. I wouldn't have thought you had it in you, but Captain Boru assures me that I would have been wrong."

And it was Maddox's turn to blush. Padraig still felt like a proud papa, watching these two get recognized for the work they'd done.

"I had a good captain training me how to do it the right way," Maddox said quietly.

"Not every young officer listens, Nevin," she replied. "I asked you to join us today because I have some pointed questions, and your answers do not have to leave this room if you choose. We're here to talk about your future."

"Mine, sir?" Maddox stammered in surprise.

Padraig had known it was coming, but Madam Gelashvili had reached out for a private—extensive—briefing on the topic when *Marrakesh* had first reached dock. She knew as much as he did, because Padraig had tried to answer every question she had asked in as much detail as he could, knowing that she would remember every word he spoke.

"I'm told by Captain Boru that you are at that point in your career where you would normally be up for a promotion both in rank and responsibilities," she continued. "The word he used, by the way, was a *crossroads.*"

She turned to smile at Nyssa, causing Padraig's Radio Officer to blush yet a third time.

In the end, that had become the term everyone had latched onto. And it had fit, because so many lives had changed as a result of a simple cargo run mission into the deepest parts of deep space.

Maddox merely nodded when she looked back at him, patiently waiting for some other shoe to drop, knowing Nevin. Silent until he needed to speak.

"Because of what *Marrakesh* does for me, we have some latitude in things, Armiger," Gelashvili nodded. "Fleet accepts that I would like to keep as much of this crew together as long as possible, understanding that normal promotion and transfer cycles are generally at odds with such things. In this instance, most of Boru's crew have at least another year before we face harder choices. However, he tells me that you might wish to transfer off of *Marrakesh*?"

Maddox flinched as if expecting a blow, but he wasn't prepared to deal with the ultimate boss today. Not really. Padraig stepped in to rescue him.

"What she's asking is where you think you might make the best contribution in the future, Maddox," he said.

Maddox nodded.

"Originally, I was disappointed not to be assigned to a warship on line duty, sir," Maddox told the First Secretary. "Dead-end gunnery officer job, at least as I saw it at the time."

"You've fought more battles than most of the cruisers I am familiar with, Nevin," she smiled.

"Aye, sir," he relaxed enough to smile back some. "And done well enough, I think."

"Better than well, Armiger," she corrected him. "Far better."

And he blushed.

"I've given a lot of thought to my future, sirs," he continued, glancing around the room. "About asking for a Gunnery Officer slot on a front-line vessel. Or a First Officer spot somewhere where we're likely to be in combat. At the same time, Captain Boru tasked me with thinking like a Survey Corps officer because this was supposed to be a mission of pure exploration. No trouble. No weapons. Just sight-seeing."

"You and your field team saw the only combat on the mission," Gelashvili pointed out.

"Aye, sir, and it was righteous, killing that damned cat before it could hurt Sotiria or Stavroula," Maddox agreed. "However, that was exploration work, and I find that I really enjoyed that part as much as I have being the Gunnery Officer on *Marrakesh*."

"So if I offered your services to Survey Corps, you might be interested?" she asked delicately.

"Sir?"

"As with Taggart, you are up for an award for how you handled that First Contact, Armiger," she turned serious now. "Survey Corps inquired with Transport Command. They spoke with Fleet. Fleet quietly reached out to me, because only a few extremely senior flag officers over there know the truth of what you folks do for me."

"Survey Corps inquired about me, sir?" Maddox gasped.

Padraig smiled. Maddox Nevin really didn't understand how different he was from the usual Gunnery Officer, all cocky and attitude. Padraig had taken the young man he'd gotten and turned Maddox Nevin a different direction.

Into who he was today.

"They have," she nodded.

"Captain mentioned that Survey Corps might be a place where I could get ahead quicker, on account that most officers would rather serve with Fleet," he said, words trailing off at that point.

"And he was correct," the First Secretary confirmed. "Those officers think there is glory in combat. I suppose that they aren't wrong, but Transport Command makes Fleet possible, because you carry the goods that keep the warfighters going. Survey Corp does a lot of things in a similar manner, working on the edges of the map, finding lost colonies occasionally, or locating worlds that can be colonized. Occasionally, they get pulled into line duty as Fleet scouts because they have the best dedicated equipment for it. Jacks of all trades, as it were. Rather like

Marrakesh has turned into for me, though that was accidental at first."

"What could I do in Survey Corps?" Maddox finally asked her, screwing his courage tight from the way his shoulders moved and his head and jaw came up.

"I haven't gotten deep into their needs and immediate details, Nevin," she replied. "It was necessary to speak with you first. But you would be interested?"

"I have found a new side of things that I didn't know I would enjoy, sir," Maddox nodded. "Sotiria and Stavroula just reinforced that."

"Which reminds me," the First Secretary said, turning and locking on Padraig as he sat up straighter. "Both of those young ladies, working through their aunt, the formidable Chrysa, and their kinswoman Galini, have petitioned to travel to *A'Zedi* and attend school. Possibly—and this might have been something lost in translation along the way—to join the Fleet. Specifically, exploration and perhaps Survey Corps."

She left it at that and Padraig nodded.

"They learned Spacer extremely quickly, First Secretary," Padraig replied. "Professor Whitlaw basically worked all day bilingually, then held classes at every meal. I'm not especially sharp at the dialect of *Riffrost* they speak, but many of my crew are. Similarly, there are a number of folks from Sabahattin that can converse reasonably well with us."

"Your doing?" she asked.

"Aye, sir," Padraig said. "My responsibility to get that world ready to talk and trade with the wider galaxy. The easiest way to do that was educational. They will likely initiate some sort of system government in another year or two, once people have covered as much of that world as possible to locate all the tribes. I got the impression that it wasn't very inhabited. Maybe a few million people combined, but that's because of the low technology level they had available."

"Are those two folks ready for modern technology?" she pressed.

Padraig paused to consider.

"Not Transport Command," he said. "Maybe Line, working initially in Security. Definitely Survey Corps, because they have extensive planetary hostile environment training and would actually be good at teaching others. Either Sotiria or Stavroula would be acceptable on *Marrakesh*, understanding that we do different things. We might not need their skills that often, but they'd be extremely helpful when it came up. And it might help draw Sabahattin deeper into our orbit, when normally they would be expected to align with *Traisa*, based on geography."

"Understood, Captain," she agreed. "My analysts said something similar when asked. We'll circle back to that later. Armiger Nevin."

Maddox snapped to, even seated.

"Sir?"

"With your permission, I'll have a few chats with some folks in Survey Corps Command," she stated. "Let's see what they might have to offer that you and I might find acceptable?"

"Sir?" he squeaked, a bit bewildered.

"Maddox Nevin, you should be rewarded for what you have accomplished, even thus far," she said with a proud smile Padraig echoed. "I don't want them wasting your talents on something stupid, merely because they have an extra warm body to use."

"I'll go where ordered, sir," Maddox assured her.

"And you will do well, wherever that is," she agreed. "I want that to be something that benefits Survey Command, Fleet, *and* Intelligence. Just because you might move over there doesn't mean you and I won't speak again, Armiger."

Padraig liked the way Maddox's eyes got big. Nyssa's smile was that of a younger sister cheering on a big brother, which honestly was the relationship those two had.

"I'll need a new Gunnery Officer, sir," Padraig spoke up, when it became clear that Maddox and Gelashvili were serious about this particular crossroads. "One with the kinds of security clearances and sharpness to understand that *Marrakesh* is really an Intelligence operation most of the time. And likely to face hostile forces."

"I have a stack of personnel files I'll transmit to you, Captain," she nodded. "We couldn't be certain where young Nevin wanted to end up, so I didn't want to jump that gun if he was solidly planted on your deck."

Padraig turned to Maddox and smiled at the young man.

"You'll do fine," Padraig told him. "And don't be a stranger, wherever duty takes you after this. It is not an ending. Merely a new opening for you, even as the rest of us continue on our paths."

"Crossroads, sir," Maddox nodded.

Padraig nodded back.

Crossroads, indeed.

READ MORE

Be sure to read the rest of the Operation Marrakesh series!

https://www.knottedroadpress.com/product-category/science-fiction/operation-marrakesh

ABOUT THE AUTHOR

Blaze Ward writes science fiction in the Alexandria Station universe (Jessica Keller, The Science Officer, The Story Road, etc.) as well as several other science fiction universes, such as Star Dragon, the Dominion, and more. He also writes odd bits of high fantasy with swords and orcs. In addition, he is the Editor and Publisher of *Boundary Shock Quarterly Magazine*. You can find out more at his website www.blazeward.com, as well as Facebook, Goodreads, and other places.

Blaze's works are available as ebooks, paper, and audio, and can be found at a variety of online vendors. His newsletter comes out regularly, and you can also follow his blog on his website. He really enjoys interacting with fans, and looks forward to any and all questions—even ones about his books!

Never miss a release!
If you'd like to be notified of new releases, sign up for my newsletter.

http://www.blazeward.com/newsletter/

Buy More!
Did you know that you can buy directly from the KRP website?

https://www.knottedroadpress.com/shop/

Connect with Blaze!

Web: www.blazeward.com
Boundary Shock Quarterly (BSQ):
https://www.boundaryshockquarterly.com/

ABOUT KNOTTED ROAD PRESS

Knotted Road Press publishes dynamic fiction set in exotic locations and unique non-fiction voices in genres such as autobiography, business, cookbooks, and how-to. Our authors cover a wide range of genres including science fiction, fantasy, mystery, literary, and poetry, appealing to all readers. We offer both DRM-free ebooks and print books for a global readership.

Knotted Road Press
www.KnottedRoadPress.com
www.KnottedRoadPress.com/Shop

www.ingramcontent.com/pod-product-compliance
Lightning Source LLC
Chambersburg PA
CBHW071527120726
47907CB00013B/1100